JORGE STAMADIANOS

BEER CANS IN THE RIO DE LA PLATA

JORGE STAMADIANOS

BEER CANS IN THE RIO DE LA PLATA

Translated by

LELAND H. CHAMBERS

.

LATIN AMERICAN LITERARY REVIEW PRESS
SERIES: DISCOVERIES
1999

The Latin American Literary Review Press publishes Latin American creative
writing under the series title Discoveries,
and critical works under the series title Explorations.

Library of Congress Cataloging-in-Publication Data:

Stamadianos. Jorge. 1961-
    [Latas de cerveza en el Río de la Plata. English]
    Beer cans in the Río de la Plata / Jorge Stamadianos; translated by
Leland H. Chambers.
        p. cm. — (Discoveries)
        ISBN 1-891270-00-1
        I. Chambers, Leland H., 1928- II. Title. III. Series.
PQ7798.29.T33L3813 1998
863—dc21   98-37804
                                                                 CIP

The paper used in this publication meets the minimum requirements of the
American National Standard for Permanence of Paper for Printed Library
Materials Z39.48-1984. ∞

Latin American Literary Review Press
121 Edgewood Avenue
Pittsburgh, PA 15218

ACKNOWLEDGMENTS

My deepest thanks to my wonderful agent Julie Popkin, who from the beginning believed in me and in BEER CANS, and who fought as valiantly as Don Quixote ever did to get it published; to Yvette Miller, who fell in love with Ulysses at first sight, thus enabling the story of his odyssey to become known in this country; to Leland H. Chambers, for having been patient enough to come up with the most adequate words to translate this troublesome Argentine slang; to Kathlean Ballew, for her knowledge and expertise in the final touches; and to my friend Ricardo Cailett-Bois, who for months was forced to dream about beer cans until he hit upon the design for the cover.

To Demetrio and Margarita,
who put me on this earth.
To Clotilde, who fell from a dream.

...Where is that man
who, the days and nights of his exile,
wandered through the world like a dog
and said that Nobody was his name?

—Jorge Luis Borges
The Odyssey, Book XXIII

1

· · · · · · · · ·

When Chris—fat Chris—takes off her bra and licks me all over the calves and then, slithering like a seal, keeps going higher as if I were some kind of an ice cream cone, the images of an avalanche, a tidal wave, a blimp falling through the void in flames burst into my mind like a set of perfect metaphors. But I pay no attention to them. I know—I've seen this coming for some time—that the only thing I can do is remember what my father used to say:

"Life is unpredictable. Any attempt to try and make something out of it isn't worth the trouble. We're nothing more than leaves cast upon the water. The best we can do—in reality, it's the only thing we can do—is let ourselves be carried along."

He also said that our whole existence is nothing but a long training session for a unique occasion. If you were able to learn from life's hard knocks, you'd be able to do battle, come out of it gracefully, and even—with luck—manage to come out a winner. But most of the time it doesn't happen that way. The situation isn't taken advantage of, and you hate yourself for having said "yes" instead of "no," or for having picked white when everything indicated that the best thing would have been to go for the black.

"The consequences are devastating," he would add. "When the opportunity is gone, you know without a doubt that nothing will change ever again, that what you've been up to that moment is what you will go on being for the rest of your days."

The fat girl is rubbing herself against my stomach trying to bring herself to orgasm, but all I can think is that this must be the occasion my father talked about so much.

I clutch at the side of the bed with all my strength; my knuckles go white, the blood stops going through my fingers. But down below, between my legs, everything is different. What a few seconds before was scarcely a fleck, an imperfection in the wall of the dam, is now turning into a crack that is widening and growing, ready to empty out the whole reservoir at one shot.

I'm coming. I can't do anything to stop it.

Always when I'm about to come I think of something else, then I concentrate on it, I look for images, and that way I can slow things down a little. But this time it's impossible. The pressure Chris puts on my friend is like those eddies in the washbasin when you pull the plug and the inertia sucks out the water. When I was a kid I used to throw cockroaches into that whirling water; it was fun to watch them struggle against the current and see them getting sucked down the drain, no matter how crazy they shook their little legs. But now...I'm the one being pulled in.

I search for the clock in the shadowy light of the cabin. The second hand is taking centuries to move from one tick to the next, and the crack, that stubborn crack, is widening slowly but constantly, like a locomotive cutting through the middle of the dam.

How many minutes have gone by since Chris...I'm losing all notion of time. My prick is about to explode but the hands on the clock are not moving. I'm coming. I can't do anything to stop it. I try to concentrate on the cockroaches, on how many legs they have. Is it six? Eight? Eighteen? My father's warning echoes through my head again and again. "The consequences are devastating. The opportunity is gone and you know for certain that nothing will change ever again. What you have been so far up to that moment you will go on being for the rest of your life."

Like a diver in search of sunken treasure, I hold my breath and squeeze my legs together trying to shut off my glands.

Chris, oblivious to all my efforts, is rocking placidly on my stomach. A drop of sweat is running slowly down her chin, glistening like a smooth caterpillar. Until that drop falls from her skin, or until it evaporates consumed by the heat from her body, I will not come. I ask God to help me, to give me strength. The drop gets to the tip of her chin and hesitates there, getting bigger and bigger. For a few seconds I think it's going to fall, that all is lost, but Chris makes a slight move and makes it slide off toward her throat.

I bite her on the arm. She thinks I'm trying to turn her on and lets out a snort. With my teeth sunk into her flesh I look over at the clock again, trying to hold myself back, but the drop moves down as slowly as I feel myself giving way. Spinning like a pearl, it manages to reach the tip of her nipple, and now it only has the void in front of it.

It falls, the dike bursts, and me, just another cockroach, I'm whirling down through the hole.

My artillery discharges. I hug Chris like a boxer going down for the count. All is lost. The ticket that was my way to a shining future flies out of my hands and falls carried by the wind in the teeth of the storm, but…What is that? What is it that resounds like thunder? I'm not sure, this is my first time with Chris…But yes! It IS the fat girl! God heard me! Chris is coming!

Her orgasms flood the cabin, one after the other, like the brakes squealing on an eighteen-wheeler in the rain. I'm screaming like a crazy man, like I'd never enjoyed anything so much in all my life. Chris, still panting, looks at me in astonishment.

"*Qué macho!*" she whispers in Spanish, sounding like a Mexican melodrama. And then in English, "I can't believe it!"

Afterward she lets her arms relax and snuggles down on my chest. Enamored of me as she is, her face still reminds me of a cow's.

"That was so good."

If I got along better with my mother, I would thank her, one by one, for all the times she hit me on the side of the head trying to convince me that English was going to help me some day.

"I liked it too," I answered her in her own language, looking right into her eyes, shifting myself over an inch or two to keep her from squashing me. "But there's something we have to talk about, Chris…I think it's best to forget what happened tonight."

My pronunciation is perfect.

"Because of Frank?" she asks.

I know it's not a good idea for me to answer.

"I'm going to talk to him, Ulysses." She looks at me a little confused. "Frank will understand."

"It's not because of Frank, Chris. He's not what worries me…"

"So?"

I don't know how I do it, but my eyes fill with tears.

"What am I going to do when you leave?" I say. "What's between us is marvelous, but…" I turn my face aside pretending not to be able to bear her seeing me this way. "Just thinking that in a few days you'll be going away and we'll never see each other again—" a soap-opera producer wouldn't have wasted a moment signing me to a contract—"it's better, even though it's painful, for us to forget what happened tonight"— I wipe a tear from my eye with my finger—"afterward it'll be worse…"

Chris swoops down on me like a collapsing building.

"I love you! Ulysses, I love you!" she kisses me intensely. "Did you think I was going to leave you behind?"

"Yes."

Relieved, she gives me a playful slap.

"No, never!"

If she had any idea how much her fingers weighed, I'm sure she would never have done that.

"But, what…Would you take me with you?" I pretended to be surprised. But I was hardly able to hide the smile that was spreading over my face like a gash.

"Of course!" the fat girl answers.

"To the United States?"

"To New York!"

She surrounds me in her arms. She kisses me on the neck.

"Chris, I love you too," I answer her, "but—what are we going to tell Frank? He's my friend too."

"Don't worry yourself about Frank, I'm going to talk to him." I feel her heavy, sweat-covered body sticking to mine, and her steady breath warming my ear. "We're going to be so happy together…"

I rest my head on her shoulder. The reflection of the moon is coming in through the porthole, making odd shapes on the ceiling of the cabin. A strange peace comes over me. The shapes vary in intensity, with a hypnotic effect on my brain. I fall asleep. I can't do anything to stop it. As Chris caresses my vertebrae one by one, pushing me all the more deeply into a heavy drowsiness, I have this stupefying vision: I see myself naked on the sheets with my arms around a large bag filled with dollar bills. Little by little the image fades out, the way it happens in those movies when they want to give the impression of time passing, and Chris's body appears in my arms once again. This time what's making her so huge is those wads and wads of bills. I shake my head to get rid of the strange thoughts and squeeze her with all my might. Even though she is Frank's girlfriend and future wife, I don't feel the slightest guilt. Isn't that odd? Maybe that's why I don't feel any remorse, because I hear him being called Frank. In the neighborhood we always used to call him Vincent, though really his name was Juan Francisco (and that's where the name "Frank" had come from). He'd been a buddy of mine years ago—more so of my brother's—and if I feel right now that nobody can blame me for having this fat girl in my arms, it's simply because Vincent owes me something that there's no making up for, not even his wife, because what Vincent owes me—something all the money in the world can't buy—is his life.

2

. . . .

It all started on the night of April 28, 1982, the day the war with Britain over the Malvinas Islands began. Vincent was in the same barracks with my brother Miguel, in the same regiment, and the next day they were being sent off to the Malvinas. I remember that my father was pouring soda water into his wine when the phone rang, and if I picked it up it was only because I was closest to it. I had just gone to the refrigerator to get some catsup to put on the steak.

"Listen to me a minute, pip-squeak," Miguel said to me the second he heard my voice.

"Who is it?" Pa asked.

"Don't tell anyone. It's me," Miguel warned me nervously.

I said it was a friend.

"Now, listen to what I'm going to tell you and don't give me any shit."

I was thirteen at the time, and the thing I did best in those days was ride my bike. The minute my brother was through telling me what I had to do, I grabbed my bicycle and raced off to help Vincent, paying no attention to my father's shouts.

When I rang the bell at his house—I'd run up the stairs two at a time because Vincent lived in a three-story building with no elevator and my brother had told me to get there as fast as I could—first I heard a series of strange sounds and then the door opened just a crack.

"Who's there?"

From the Galician accent, I knew the person on the other side of the door could only be Vincent's father.

"It's me, Ulysses," I answered. "Juan Francisco isn't here?"

"No."

"For sure?"

Vincent's father poked his nose out.

"What's the matter?" he asked, raising an eyebrow.

"Miguel called the house and said that Juan Francisco escaped and that he was coming here because it seems that in the barracks they've already found out and they're coming to look for him here, so if he comes, be sure and tell him to get away because if they see him they're going to drag him back by the scruff of his neck."

I said it all so quickly that when I was done there wasn't any breath left in me.

"When did he call?" he asked me, alarmed, grabbing my arms.

"Probably half an hour ago."

"Shit!" he shouted. "Why didn't you say so before?"

The lights were all turned out in the apartment, but since I had been there hundreds of times before, I'd memorized where all the furniture was.

"You've got to get out of here right now," the father yelled. "They've found out and are coming to look for you."

Vincent was in his underwear, standing beside the bed, and when he saw me through the door, he looked at me like he'd seen a ghost.

"Ulysses!" he exclaimed. "What're you doing here?"

"What do you mean, what's he doing here? What do you mean?" the Galician repeated, a fat vein popping out on his forehead. "Ulysses came to let us know that you're in danger, son."

The big painting that Vincent had been working on just before getting drafted was tossed on the bed together with a pile of brushes and tubes of paint. The top had come off the blue and the paint was slowly seeping out, staining the sheet.

"Miguel called home," I said, just to be saying something. "Because it looks like the barracks..."

Wow! When they heard the word "barracks," everyone stopped dead in their tracks, petrified: Vincent with his skin all goose-bumps, his father with that vein throbbing, his mother like a wax doll with her mouth open saying "Oh!", and Mirenjuli, his sister, holding out an ironed shirt stiffly as if she too were a doll. The only thing moving was the paint that kept on oozing out of the tube. I was scared because if nobody moved, the soldiers were going to get there and we'd all still be dreaming. But fortunately Vincent's father came to life and clapped his hands sharply and woke everybody up.

"Quick, son! Quick! Your pants!" The father was trying to help Vincent who was acting like a robot.

"I need to take some money with me," Vincent was still in his underpants but he was sweating nonetheless.

"Those dollars, the ones you've been saving, girl..." the mother shouted.

Mirenjuli shot out of the room like an arrow. Vincent pulled the sheet off the bed, put the big painting in the middle, and put another one on top of it, a smaller one that was already framed, then wrapped the two of them together.

"What are you doing with that?" the father shot out.

"One to finish, the other to sell if I need money."

"Leave all that shit now, they're coming to get you!" The vein in his forehead looked as if it were about to burst.

"String, Mama," ordered Vincent.

"String?"

"To tie up the paintings!"

His mother slipped out of the room wringing her hands. A few seconds later Mirenjuli appeared with her dollars, and immediately afterward the mother returned with a bag full of string. When they finished tying up the paintings, Vincent arranged the bundle on his back as if it were a backpack.

He hugged Mirenjuli first, and then his father. When he hugged his mother I thought they would never come unstuck.

"Let's go, son." His father ran his hand over Vincent's shoulder the way you would pet a cat. "No time for sentimental stuff now."

We'd just gotten to the bottom of the stairway, ready to go out into the street, when Vincent remembered something and ran up again.

"You should be a long way away from here by now!"

Even though I couldn't see the face on the Galician because I'd stayed down below waiting on a lower floor, I heard his voice echoing through the stairwell and I imagined that vein wiggling on his forehead like a worm that didn't want to get put on the hook.

"Don't you understand that if they find you we'll lose you?"

"Hide my uniform, Papa." It wasn't bad what Vincent had remembered. "So they won't know I was here."

Vincent went ahead, with his paintings on his back, and I followed him at a trot carrying the bike. When we went around the corner—not even half a block from the building—Vincent pushed me hard against one of the walls.

"Don't make a sound," he warned me, clapping his hand over my mouth.

At first I thought he was playing around, but when I saw one of those green army trucks with huge wheels coming full speed down the street, I got really quiet.

A bunch of soldiers got down off the truck and the one who seemed to be in charge started shouting. I recognized Miguel instantly, though he was wearing a helmet and boots and carrying a rifle.

The guy who'd been giving the orders took out his pistol and went into the building. Everybody followed him except my brother, who instead of paying attention to him hid behind a car and then ran over to where we were, leaping the way they do in the movies.

"I saw you from up there…" he was panting heavily. He was thin, with pimples on his face and his hair so short it made his head look bigger than it really was. "I warned the little asshole just in time," he said to Vincent, showing his teeth.

I didn't care if my brother called me a little asshole because I knew he didn't really mean it. As long as he'd let me take a couple of shots with the rifle they'd given him in the barracks…But wow! When I ask him that he almost kills me!

"Cut that shit out and go on home!"

When he saw I wasn't listening to him he came charging at me, enraged. I ran off, dropping the bicycle, and it was just our luck that it fell against a "No Parking" sign and set off an unholy racket.

A soldier who had stayed behind on guard heard the noise. He turned his head toward where we were and all three of us clearly heard it when he cocked his rifle. Vincent went nuts. He grabbed my brother by the arm and me by the neck and started pushing us toward the empty lot where we used to play ball. Now they were putting up a building there. All around the place were piles of sand, bags of cement, and heaps of those hollow bricks. Vincent and my brother hid behind a stack of cement bags, and I was behind a huge pile of bricks with my bike. Through one of the little holes I saw the soldier on the other side of the board fence, looking through it. He had a thick mustache and he looked a lot bigger than the others. Maybe he wasn't just a soldier, maybe he was a sergeant. The thing was that this guy pulled back one of the boards and was staring at the pile of bricks where I was. Could he have seen the bicycle? I looked over to see where my brother was. Vincent's eyes were closed, and he was clenching his teeth. Miguel had his hands over his head and was breathing with his mouth open, like a fish. All three of us were like we thought a bomb was going to fall any minute.

The sergeant walked around a pile of sand as if he suspected there was someone on the other side of it. I saw him very clearly through the little holes between my bricks, just as I saw the black cat when it leaped from the second floor and landed right on the pile of cement bags.

As the cat was flying through the air, the sergeant realized that something strange was moving behind him, but he didn't know what it was; as for me, I nearly shit in my pants, because he turned around so fast that he lost his footing—he didn't see that the ground was covered with rocks—and skidded and came down in the mud. He fell on his ass, it must have hurt him, right into a pool of water with a loose mixture of cement. It was probably the rage he was in when he saw what his pants looked like that made him shoot. The cat's head sailed cleanly through the air, and Vincent and my brother, hidden on the other side of the pile of cement bags, didn't know what was going on.

Grumbling to himself and shaking the mud off his pants and coughing from the dust that the bullet had spread around, the sergeant went over to the cement bags to see what was left of the cat: just a lot of fur plastered all over the cement bags, and blood. Blood and bits of flesh everywhere. The sergeant looked around a little more and spat on the ground—the dust must have gotten into his mouth. Damned if he didn't miss seeing Vincent and my brother entirely! Afterward, as if nothing at all had happened, he left, slipping through the same boards he'd come through.

"Are you all right?" my brother asked Vincent, with his teeth chattering.

"Yeah. And you?"

"More or less."

"What happened to you?' Vincent seemed scared.

"Well, nothing serious," Miguel answered. Even where I was I could smell shit. "But I think I did something…"

"What do you mean? Did you shit?"

My brother nodded.

"What are you laughing at, asshole?" Miguel pushed him. But Vincent—I think it was just nerves—couldn't stop laughing.

3

. . . .

Chris is still there, her arms around my neck and all her corpulence spilling over my body like a red hot anvil, but try as I might, I can't keep from thinking about Miguel. About the way destiny has linked together a whole series of unusual and imperceptible events through the years, pushing me, with hardly any possibility of avoiding it, into the exact spot I am right now…It's all connected. Only now—with Chris warming up my ear with the rhythm of her breathing—like in a film, am I able to see my life winding itself up again and watch it all unfold. The origin of it all, the seed that sprouted later to put me here curled up on the bed with this fat girl, was planted that night, the night of the escape, the night when Vincent, like a bottle rocket exploding, disappeared before our very eyes, carrying his paintings with him.

My brother found a spigot with a thin thread of water dripping out of it and wet a rag to clean off his butt and legs. I am never going to forget that face, that expression of humiliation he had when he threw the shit-smeared underpants against the pile of bricks. After he'd put his pants on again, we went up to the second floor of the building and jumped from there to the roof of a shed, a warehouse for the bottling plant where they kept empty jugs and bottles. Through a hole in the wire fence we came out into a dead-end that was next to the railroad tracks. Looking for the darker streets, we got to the plaza in front of the cathedral and went down into the ravine.

There was no one in the streets, no cars either, and Vincent had told us, without giving any reason why, that it was best to head for the river.

From the bottom of the ravine you couldn't see the boats, but the arms of the cranes poked up over the treetops, and as we got closer I could hear the steel cables hitting up against the masts of the sailboats. The clouds, black and fat as hogs, covered the sky threateningly, and the smell of water and damp earth was in the air, the smell you get right before a storm breaks out.

Miguel shouted at me several times to go back home, but I paid no attention. I just kept following them with the bike, staying a few yards back and listening to what they were saying.

"You gonna tell me what the hell we came down here for?"

Miguel had already asked this same question about eighty times, but the only thing Vincent would say was, "Keep following me."

It really pissed me off, this business of someone giving orders and everyone else obeying, but judging by my brother's reaction, I wasn't the only one.

"How come you don't ever open your yap, fat ass?" Tired of not getting an answer, Miguel had hung the rifle over his shoulder and now, grabbing it by the strap, he kept shaking it at him. "You gonna tell me what we came down to the river for?"

When Vincent finally gave him an answer, Miguel was still obstinate.

"Where you wanna go?" he asked incredulously.

Vincent started walking and Miguel had to trot faster to keep up with him.

"Where?" he asked again.

"Spain!" Vincent was taking long, sure steps. "My parents are going back. My grandfather owns a lot of land there."

"And how're you gonna manage to get to Spain?"

"On a plane."

"But don't you know you're a deserter, that they're not gonna let you leave the country?"

My brother looked like one of those cartoon characters that keep running in circles around someone more intelligent, insisting on getting some answers.

"A plane from Uruguay," Vincent explained. "Not from here."

"It's just the same," my brother's face was getting redder and redder. "How're you gonna manage to get to Uruguay?"

"Rowing."

"Rowing where?"

"To Uruguay!"

Miguel stopped him, grabbing him by the arm.

"Are you fuckin' with me or being serious?"

I had to get closer to hear what they were saying. A strong breeze came up and pushed their words away toward the river.

"It's no more than sixty kilometers to Uruguay, and if the river's quiet it's easy," Vincent had his paintings slung over his back as he walked along backward like a crab. "It's just empty beaches over there, the only thing you have to do is go along the coast."

"What do you mean, the coast? You have to cross the river before you get to Uruguay!"

We had reached the port, and the river, the way the water was slamming up against the concrete pilings, wasn't promising anything good for the next few minutes.

"You can go along the coast. There are places where the water doesn't get above your knees," Vincent persisted.

Stopping in front of the first sailboat in the long row that ended where the dock ended, now Vincent was the one running around my brother, trying to convince him.

"What else you gonna do, then? Go back to the barracks?" Whenever my brother didn't know what to do, one side of his face would start twitching. "What you gonna tell them? That you went to take a piss? They're gonna beat the shit out of you and then send you to the spot where the first bomb the British drop is gonna explode. And then they're gonna dump you in with the rest of the shitheads—only you're gonna be in little pieces!"

My brother walked down the bank, sat down at the edge of the water, and covered his face with his helmet. When I heard him weeping, I almost felt like sitting down beside him and putting my arms around him. But the bastard would have started yelling at me. He always did that. Whenever something turned out badly for him, he would make up some excuse and start beating on me. And if I wasn't there he would break something and then tell the old man it was my fault.

"We have to swipe a boat and get out of here, Miguel, that's the only thing we have left." My brother moved the helmet aside, and his eyes were like a couple of tangerines. "We have to get over to the other side before the sun comes up."

While Vincent kept hammering away at him, my brother got up and blew his nose on his sleeve. When he saw me still there, he freaked out and came at me running.

"What the hell are you still doing here?" he yelled.

I knew he might start something with me any second, so I got on my bike as fast as I could and pedaled until he got tired and couldn't run anymore. But when he stopped, the son of a bitch picked up some rocks and started throwing them at me.

"Don't you realize the folks are gonna get worried, you little piece of shit?" I dodged all the rocks. "Get back home!"

"But what are you gonna do?"

"What the fuck do you care what I'm gonna do, asshole?"

In the meantime Vincent had gotten on board one of the sailboats and was untying a dinghy.

"Tell me what you're gonna do!"

"Get out of here," screamed my brother.

"Where you gonna go?"

Vincent pulled up closer to us, rowing between two of the sail-boats.

"Let's go, Miguel," he shouted when he got to the water's edge.

My brother dropped the rocks he had ready to throw at me and sat down on the bank like he was going to jump into the boat, but before getting in he called out to me, as if he were giving me one last chance.

"If you wanna go with us, come on."

"Go where?"

I was sure my brother was playing nice just to get me to come closer so he could start beating on me.

"You coming or not?"

"You gonna hit me if I come?"

"No, I ain't gonna do nothing."

I went closer, still perched on the bike, ready to get out of there.

"Where we gonna go?" I asked them from a few yards away.

"Hurry up!" was the only thing my brother said, and he got up like he wanted me to go first. I didn't like that move, so I put my foot on the pedal and turned the bike around. He started to run so I started pedaling again.

"You piece of shit, if you don't go home I swear I'm gonna grab you off that bicycle and throw it in the river. Listen to me."

He threw one last rock at me and then got into the boat. When I saw them heading out into the channel, behind the line of boats, I went close to the water's edge and followed them along the dock. They were seated in the middle, both of them, and each one was pushing an oar. In the bow of the dinghy, the paintings wrapped in the sheet gleamed like glowworms every time the beam from the lighthouse passed over them.

When the row of boats came to an end the dock turned into a break-water made of rocks and rubbish, and I had to go under a wire fence and leave my bike behind in order to follow them. There was a lot of trash, rusty wire, and old tin cans among the rocks, and a terrible smell like something was dead. The wind was stronger and the waves were higher. Vincent stopped rowing to settle the paintings into the bow better and my brother took advantage of the moment to hit at the bottom of the boat with the heel of his shoe. He did it several times, distrustful, until Vincent stared at him to ask him what he was doing.

"The water's not gonna get in from there?"

Vincent looked down to where my brother was pointing.

"Why? What's the matter?"

"Oh, nothing…But it's just made of wood."

"What else is a boat going to be made of if it's not wood, Miguel?"

As his only reply, my brother grabbed his oar and sank it deep into the water, testing how deep it was.

"This shit sure moves a lot."

I was walking over the rocks, trying to keep up while they rowed toward the mouth of the river. The wind was making the words that reached me seem half cut off, almost unintelligible; I had to really try to make out what they were saying. Suddenly lightning lit up the river and the wind really started to blow, a clear warning that in a few minutes the storm would be at full blast.

"Miguel!"

He didn't answer me. He always did that. When he couldn't hit me, he acted like he was the one who was hurt.

"Miguel!" I called out again.

"What's wrong with you, you little asshole?"

"Are you really going?" The beam of light from the lighthouse swept over them. "Mama's gonna be mad if you go away."

"Asshole, don't you know when to shut up?" He let go of the oar and stood up so abruptly that he almost turned the boat over.

"When are you gonna come back?"

"Go on home!"

I had gotten too close to where the rocks sank into the water and the waves were getting my shoes wet but I didn't care. I was nervous and started crying.

"Tell me where you're going," I screamed in desperation. Every time I opened my mouth, the pitch of my voice got higher. "When are you gonna come back?" My legs folded up under me and I had to sit down on top of a rusty boiler to keep from falling. "What am I gonna tell Mama?"

When Miguel saw me crying, he covered his face up with his hands. Vincent was shaking his head; he couldn't believe what he was seeing.

"What's the matter now?"

"The little asshole's right…" Miguel was sobbing. "What am I gonna do in Spain? Send my old lady a postcard from there? She'd die if I left."

"Forget your old lady, you dumb shit!" The waves were shaking the boat as if they might turn it over. "They're gonna send you to the front. You're the one who's gonna have to go to war!"

"But you've got some uncles there, cousins…What am I gonna do?"

Vincent seized both of the oars and with a couple of strokes by himself brought the boat up close to the rocks. The waves were beating it against the breakwater but my brother was in no hurry to get out.

"You understand what I'm telling you?" Vincent didn't want to look at him. "If I send a postcard to my old lady from Spain she's gonna have a heart attack."

When Miguel jumped onto the rocks, I got up off the boiler just in case it might occur to that son of a bitch to start beating on me. I still had the salty taste of tears on my cheeks.

Rowing harder now, Vincent drew away from the breakwater. My brother followed him along the shoreline, stumbling over the rocks, without realizing that Vincent was rowing faster and faster now and that it was too hard to catch up.

"Vincent! Vincent!" he called out, almost screaming.

But Vincent was already in the open river. He had just left the protection of the breakwater and now the little boat was shaking about on the surface of the water, almost uncontrollable. He had to plunge the oars in deep in order to cut through the waves and keep from capsizing.

Miguel, standing on the last rock facing the immense expanse of water, cupped his hands over his mouth so his words would carry in the wind.

"I didn't mean to shit on you!"

Vincent shouted something back at him, but the thunder got in the way and devoured his words.

"What?" shouted my brother. "What did you say?"

Vincent brought his hands up to his mouth to protect himself against the wind. This time we heard him. But his voice sounded distant, far away, as if Vincent were already another person, as if the three of us were all in a dream, a nightmare.

"You got no balls, Miguel!"

Like an antipersonnel mine going off unexpectedly in a minefield, a burst of lightning broke out over the river.

"No balls…" was heard like an echo.

Then an electric ray split the sky in two, separating my brother from me forever, and me from Vincent, and Vincent and my brother from each other.

4

. . . .

Ten years went by. We never saw either of them again. Neither alive nor dead. The world had swallowed Vincent, and the earth my brother. I was twenty-three years old, I'd be twenty-four soon, and I didn't know what to do with my life. My only goal—pursued with a compulsiveness that had made me uncontrollable in those last months—was to get drunk, to get away from any part of the world around me.

It was a Friday night, as oppressive a Friday night as any other. We had drunk some beers, Martín and I, and we kept on drinking slowly as we got closer to downtown. Martín was saying that now, with the Citroën, the chicks would throw themselves on top of us like flies. I went along with him, not to burst his bubble. But down deep I was convinced it would be the same as always—driving around, following some chick that wouldn't give us any, finishing off the night eating pizza in some filthy dive until the beer finally got us down. But I wasn't complaining. Stale as these occasions were, it was much better than staying at home and putting up with my parents. For some time now they had been in the habit of coming down on me because I hadn't done anything all day. But I wasn't anybody's slave; I wasn't going to work my ass off even to fart, just so they could get a couple of bucks out of me.

It must have been around two in the morning when we got to the Avenida Cabildo. People were piled up around the lighted storefront windows of the shops and the cars were moving very slowly, almost in a caravan. Martín took advantage of the opportunity to stick his arm out the window and show off his muscles; three months ago, when it first began to get hot, he started going to the gym every day. I didn't have the bread to go to the gym but just the same I was killing myself up on the rooftop, doing sit-ups and push-ups, and then I would collapse on the flagstones for awhile; and when the sun really started coming down I would get into the Pelopincho, the wading pool we had up there.

We were stopped at a signal light, proudly showing off our bodies, when Martín punched me in the ribs.

"Look at that redhead," he said, poking his finger up against the windshield.

Standing with the crowd as if waiting for someone, a redhead was chewing gum, moving her jaw vigorously. She had on black pantyhose that showed off her beautifully shaped legs, a denim vest, and clogs. And as far as I'm concerned, there is nothing in this universe that turns me on faster than a chick wearing clogs. I saw myself stretched out over her like a spider, her white skin starting to raise up on contact with my tongue, and I couldn't help but notice that something in my pants was getting hard.

"Really hot!" I commented, all excited.

Martín was completely gone, in a coma. The reason the redhead had stopped there was to wait for an amazing blonde who had just gotten a light from a bald-headed fellow nearby and was now walking back very leisurely, in slow motion, blowing the smoke out sensually through her mouth. I bet she sunbathed in the nude, too, because her body was totally bronze—ragged jeans with a hole about where her ass showed a piece of cheek that was undeniable proof—and the curvy blonde seemed about to be busting out all over; unlike the redhead, who was flat-chested, her breasts were huge. When they saw we were staring at them with our eyes stuck to the windshield like snails, the redhead turned her eyes away, but the blonde exhaled provocatively and riveted her eyes on us.

"What do we do?" Martín was suddenly nervous.

The light turned green, and the cars behind us started signaling with their lights for us to get a move on.

"Go ahead?"

The driver of the bus we had right behind us started honking.

"Should I go and turn around?"

I didn't know how to answer him. Martín put it in first and was about to let the clutch out when I stopped him, gripping him by the arm.

"If we go around again we'll lose them."

The blonde noticed the cars signaling us with their lights and the bus honking and she nearly busted out of her buttons laughing.

"We can't stay here all day, shithead!"

"Wait a second."

"The guys behind me are going to beat the shit out of us if I don't go."

Urged on by the beer flooding through my brain, I pulled back the Citroën's sunroof and poked half my body up through it.

"What's the matter with you?" I shouted at the driver, totally out of control. "You're breaking your balls with that horn! What's your problem? Is your old lady waiting for you?"

Encouraged by the prospect of bloodshed, a group of idiots standing in front of one of the store windows turned around.

"Fight! Fight!" a skinny guy was shrieking.

The driver behind me stuck his head out of the window.

"I'm gonna push that tin bucket against the lamp post and grind you to shit, asshole!"

"It's in the middle of the goddamn night on a Saturday, you shithead. These people have had it up to here with your fucking horn honking all week long!"

An old woman walking by with her dog applauded. "The kid's right," she chimed in.

"How come you're getting into this, lady?" the bus driver shouted.

I don't know how the discussion went from there because I turned to face the chicks.

"I'll do anything for you, sweethearts." There I was, standing up like on stage with a bottle of beer in my hand and everyone looking at me. "But this car belongs to my friend and it would be a shame if they bump into it; he just bought it yesterday."

The blonde looked at me in a roguish sort of way.

"So what's it to us?"

When she crossed her arms her tits shot out like a couple of watermelons. "Would you say that to the bald guy's wife?"

"What bald guy?" she asked, taken aback.

"The one you just got a light from." I pretended to be looking for him in the crowd. "Look," I said, pointing toward an imaginary spot. "He just had a heart attack, he's delirious, he says he just saw some flying saucers…" The blonde was laughing but I was just getting worked up. "His wife's calling for an ambulance. You have to go over and tell them what really happened, they'll put the poor guy in an insane asylum if you don't."

The bus's horn plus the driver's yelling were pounding at my ears, but it was useless, nothing could stop me, I'd managed to get the blonde's attention and now I was going to follow her to the end.

"Watermelons! The man is asking for watermelons!" I was making like a clown.

The bus driver, tired of all the gibing and hooting, was ready to drive right over us like a rooster in a henyard. He put it in first and came up against us, his bumper right against ours.

"Are you going to let him flatten us?"

The Citroën was shaking, leaning to one side.

"Let's go around the block, Ulysses." Martín was trembling.

"They drive like they were herding cattle," screamed the old lady.

The son of a bitch bus driver accelerated a couple more times, threatening finally to really sink us altogether. I started laughing like a maniac.

"That orangutan is gonna make mincemeat out of us if you don't get in!"

On a desperate impulse, Martín opened the back door, which wobbled back and forth like a circus clown in a fit of bowing, and begged them to get in. "He's gonna shit all over us, girls! Please."

Wet around the armpits, sweating in huge drops like a pot full of boiling water, Martín put it in gear and started up at the exact moment the bus began to push us out into the flow of cars going across the intersection after the light had turned red again. Overjoyed with such a good catch—the chicks had finally gotten in the car—we got out of there, turning full speed down one of the side streets, but not before having to swallow the abuse coming from all the cars we'd made to slam on their brakes.

5

· · · · · · · · ·

Martín, that son of a bitch, was having a fantastic time. He'd grabbed the blonde, who was a goddess, and they parked the Citro in the scrub near the lake. Even from where I was I could hear them making enough noise to raise the dead. On the other hand, with the redhead everything had gone from bad to worse. I hadn't even started to get my hand in when the bitch cut me off, saying she felt a little sick. It was her fault we were stuck there, the two of us staring into each other's face with nothing to do, nothing to say to each other.

"You wanna go somewhere?"

"My boyfriend is waiting for me."

"How come you got in the car if you had a boyfriend?"

She didn't even answer.

"It's really interesting talking to you, you know? Up shit creek."

No answer.

Over by the trees the Citro went on rocking back and forth rhythmically, and I thought I would go mad if I didn't do something.

"You could have told me beforehand that you were feeling sick, couldn't you?"

"Don't be so rude, just..."

She was right, but I left her there so I wouldn't have to start telling her off. I walked a few yards away, into the trees, trying to get away from those sounds that did nothing else but point up my own failure, when a strange noise, something like a balloon popping, made me turn around, unsuspecting. Damn! The door to the Citroën had sprung open and I could see everything they were doing. The blonde was naked, her hands resting on the car seat. Martin was shoving at her from behind like a wild dog. Her tits were shaking back and forth like bunches of grapes. And the white band from her bikini made her golden nipples stand out all the more clearly. It would have taken more than Martín's two hands to get around them! As it happened, they realized what had happened right away and shut the door even before my head snapped around like a cork out of a champagne bottle. That vision had lasted so briefly, it had been so fleeting, that for a moment I even doubted it, I didn't know if what I 'd seen was real or if it was my imagination. I hadn't been with a woman in so long it wouldn't have been strange for me to be hallucinating.

"Why don't we go someplace else and leave them alone?"

That stupid bitch's remark let me know that what I'd seen wasn't the fruit of my imagination. She must have followed me because she was afraid to be left alone, but to me—in the grip of desperation due to abstinence—she appeared to be a little more docile than before, anxious to be a little more friendly. I went closer to her with my best smile, ready to forgive her and start new.

"I'd be delighted to leave them alone, but…what do you want me to do? I'm not made of steel, and as long as I can't do anything on top of you…"

"You can't win all the time," she said, pulling her gum out only to pop it back into her mouth again.

"Win, no…But no one should be denied having a little fun…"

You can imagine the sour face that bitch pulled when she turned away offended. Martín wasn't going to let me forget this. My only salvation was to go at her from another angle. I waited awhile until I thought she was feeling better and went up to her again, this time determined to go all the way. She had taken a fresh piece of gum out of her purse— there was a whole bubble gum factory in there—and was chewing at about four hundred times a second.

"What's your name again?" I asked her.

"Silvana."

I got a little closer and leaned one hand against the tree. With the other I played with the ends of her hair.

"You know, Silvana, there are other things we could do all the same. You know, even though you're not ready, things that could be almost the same…"

She stopped chewing abruptly and looked me up and down.

"Exactly what are you thinking?"

"Come on, now…what's it gonna hurt you?" I got even closer and put my arm around her waist trying to come off affectionate. "How about a kiss…"

The redhead fixed me with a look so full of hate that I was certain anything I tried now would lead to disaster, without fail.

But I was desperate. "Why not?" I shouted. "We're all alone here, your friend is having a fabulous time with my buddy—so what's the problem?"

"Because I don't want to. I don't like you." Still chewing away at that cud, she looked me over with disgust.

"How come you don't like me?"

"I just don't like you, you're ugly, I wouldn't do anything with you…"

"If I'm so ugly, why the fuck did you get into the car?"

She stared at me in silence for a few seconds and then, it was her whole reply, shrugged her shoulders. "I was bored."

That poor bitch couldn't even put together a good excuse.

While Martín drove I tried to get myself back together. To keep from hitting the redhead, I'd walked off to a little open-air stand at the other end of the lake. I don't remember how long I was there, it could have been hours or simply minutes, but when Martín appeared he had to pull out his wallet and pay for the last beers because I'd drunk so much I didn't have any money left.

"This country is a bucket of shit!" The wind was beating in my face now and I was shouting in Martín's ear from just inches away, clutching the back of the car seat to keep from falling. "A rotten turd of a place where we're all screwed up and no one knows it!"

"What the hell are you shouting in my ear for, you dumb shit? Are you out of your fucking mind?" Pissed off, he turned around and with a blow of his fist knocked me down.

"Everyone's hysterical around here!"

A family inside of a car with its roof covered with suitcases had to put up with my drunken face sticking my tongue out at them.

"Fistfuckers! Lunatics! It's all your fault!" I looked at the one who must have been the father. "It's you I'm talking to, you son of a bitch. What the hell are you teaching your children?"

Martín fixed it somehow to force me to stick my head back in, but it didn't last long. He had to take care of the steering wheel to keep us from running into a streetlight, so I made the most of it and went back to the window.

"My balls are aching from jacking off so much!"

I climbed up on the seat and started screaming, grabbing at my crotch.

"I want some chick to come and rape me!"

Martín chose to slow down. The car with the family soon got way ahead of us.

"What's the matter with you, you dumb shit? You want them to take us away on a stretcher?"

"You think that shit about the redhead was for real? You think she was serious?" I got so angry thinking about it that the only way to get it off my chest was to shout. "It's a lie! She wasn't on the fucking rag!"

"Stop shouting in my ear!" Martín didn't know what to do anymore to shut me up.

"She's just hysterical! Like everyone else! They tell you they don't have any dough but the bills are just falling out of their purses! They tell you they have to work hard when they spend the whole day scratching their balls! They tell you you have to go to school but later on you can't find a job anywhere!"

I was about to go on spewing all the ideas the alcohol had so lucidly put in my brain when suddenly the taste of acid leaped up from the pit of my stomach, flooding my mouth. I started coughing and then retching. Martín turned and threatened me with his finger.

"I'll beat the shit out of you if you puke in here!"

I stuck my head out the window and, like a cataract, hurled everything I had drunk out onto the hot pavement.

6

· · · · · · · · ·

While the blonde was taking my pants down, the redhead got her hand
inside the fly and fondled me. Through half-closed eyes I saw her take
out my cock and put it in her mouth. The blonde, meanwhile, was rubbing my balls with her velvet hands. Her head, flush against the redhead's,
gazed up at me longingly: she also wanted a taste of it.

"Both of you, girls, both…" I encouraged them as my eyes were
losing focus, "at the same time."

I shut my eyes to give myself over completely to the moistness of
their tongues, when suddenly it all began to whirl around as if they had
tossed me into a centrifuge. Something awful, howling like a hyena,
was coming down over me. When I opened my eyes I was striking at the
air with my fists. The screeching was coming from an alarm clock Mama
was always hiding somewhere to keep me from destroying it. I leaped
out of bed determined to tear it apart but the sheets were still wrapped
around my legs and I fell on my face. With my cheek against the floor,
aching from the blow, I listened to that piece of shit yammering away
from some hidden spot in the room. With a tug I got the sheets off and
started the search. By feeling underneath the bed I found it. When I
pulled it out the god damn thing was shaking in my hand as if it were alive.
This was a new one, with two little bronze bells above the face and a
hammer in between them that was shaking frantically back and forth.
With a single jerk I raised my arm back and smashed it against the blinds.

I went out to the patio in my bathing suit. The way the sun was
bouncing off the walls it must have been almost noon. I had to go back
to my room and look for my sunglasses; I could hardly see for all the
glare. The protection of the smoked glass together with the cold tiles
under my feet helped to reduce the throbbing in my head.

The smell of chicken was coming from the kitchen. My sister
Jorgelina was sitting down reading next to the open door, and Ma was
drying the plates. As they had been doing for a while now, neither one of
them addressed me with even a word. My sister would grope for some

food on her plate and when she found it she would put it in her mouth. She was two years younger than me and always looked a little dirty. You could see it in her hair especially, because it floated around her face like a cloud of flies. She was engaged to a fat guy with pimples all over his face. She called him Toti. It always disgusted me when I saw them together, so much that I didn't want to think about it anymore, because if I did I would lose my appetite.

"Anything to eat?" I asked, rubbing my eyes.

"No," Mama replied without even looking around at me.

"Nothing?"

Total silence. I took a couple of steps and sat down facing my sister.

"What happened?" I asked again. "Did our beloved little pig eat it all up?"

My sister's face turned red and looked sour, and she buried herself in her book again. I opened the oven door. On the rack there was a plate with a couple of pieces of chicken and some potatoes.

"And who is this for?"

"For your father!" Ma shut the door with a kick of her slippered foot.

"There's no food for me?"

"In this house there will be no more food for you!" She was drying the plates so vigorously I was afraid she'd throw them at my head any minute. "What time did you get home last night?"

My stupid sister stopped reading and looked at me in disgust.

"Your father went to wake you up this morning and you were still so drunk you didn't even know who was speaking to you!"

Whenever Mama got mad at me she would shout at me in Greek. I understood it perfectly—we had all learned it when we were kids—but I still couldn't avoid getting worked up every time I heard it. Anything, even the stupidest reproaches, sounds really tragic in that language.

"Come on, Mama, don't get on my case," I said, trying to calm her down. "It was Friday night…"

But she threw the dishtowel down and ran out of the kitchen sobbing, dragging her slippers on the patio tiles. "I never thought a son of mine would turn out like this! Never!"

My sister was looking at me, biting her lip, shaking her head like she thought I was sick and hopeless.

"And what's the matter with you, shithead? Why are you looking at me like that?"

Since she wouldn't answer me I reached over and stole a drumstick. I didn't do it because I was hungry—Mama had taken away any appetite I might have had—but because it irritated me that Jorgelina was giving me that superior look. But she threw herself on me like a tiger.

"Give me that!"

With my arm stretched out and my hand over her face it was impossible for her to get any closer.

"Mama!" she started squealing like a pig. "Mama!"

I let out a fart. It smelled so awful, even I couldn't believe it. Jorgelina moved back frightened like she had seen a ghost. She rolled up the newspaper and beat me on the head, while with the other hand she held her nose so she wouldn't have to breathe. But the smell must have been really bad because after a few seconds she couldn't take any more and went out of the kitchen, wretching and gagging. I farted again, a big one to let her know what was waiting for her if she came back. Then I sat down at the table to finish off what was left on her plate—hardly any potatoes and one piece of chicken. It was a little disgusting to think that my sister's fingers had been poking around in it, but my hunger had come back full force and there was nothing else in sight.

When I finished eating I thought about going back to bed for a siesta, but it was so hot in the room I finally climbed up to the rooftop terrace to get into the Pelopincho, the wading pool. My old man had bought it for the three of us when we were kids. Miguel was ten or twelve when they brought it home and he'd helped Pa fill it up. Above the television there's a snapshot where you see him holding the garden hose while my sister and I are screaming with joy, clinging to an inflated duck. Now the Pelopincho has so many patches you can hardly tell what the original was made out of.

I sat down first so the sun would get me all warm before plunging in. With the relaxing feeling of knowing that nobody was going to come and bother me—Jorgelina couldn't come out in the sun because she'd always get a big rash, and my parents would never come up here—I closed my eyes trying to get back to the erotic dream I'd been having that morning, but no matter how hard I tried, the images were too hazy and confused. The redhead ran off into the trees and the one who came back was Martín, rolling up his shirtsleeves with the obvious intention of slugging me. I shook my head to try and put things back in their place but a shrill voice from the house next door scattered them.

"Are you washing something down there now, Mama?"

"Just the dishes."

"Why do you have to wash them now? There's no water up here!"

If I wasn't mistaken, that was Miriam's voice.

"I'm done now, sweetheart."

And the shrill voice answering her from afar belonged to her mother, Luisa. My parents and hers had known each other since before we were born. Miriam's father had had a hardware store but things had gone bad for him and he'd had to sell it. When we were kids we'd been close friends, and we'd even gone to a private tutor together for math, but lately I hadn't seen her for some time.

"Mama, I'm burning up!"

To see what was going on on the other side of the dividing wall, I had to climb up on the upturned canoe. I stepped carefully because I didn't want to put a hole in it. It had been sitting on those sawhorses for so long I was afraid the fiberglass might have dried out and would give way. But when I set my foot on top of it, it just caved in a little. It was holding. Years before I had spent whole days in it, but later on the river got contaminated by all the shit the factories were emptying out into the water and ended up full of dead fish. At low tide, there was a rotten smell all over the place.

On the other side of the wall, Miriam was standing next to the handrail of the terrace overlooking the patio—her house and mine were practically the same—wearing a yellow bikini and holding a garden hose.

"What's all the shouting over there?" I asked her.

"Mama hasn't shut off the faucet down below," she answered matter-of-factly. I didn't call attention to the fact that I was barely hanging there, nor that we hadn't seen each other for a long time.

"Mama, could you hurry, please?"

She didn't have a very good ass but her tits had grown considerably since the last time we'd seen each other.

"What's going on down there, nothing's coming out, Mama?"

Miriam let go of the hose and went over toward the banister in little hops, lifting her feet off the tiles as if they were being scorched.

"You're unbearable, Miriam!" Luisa's voice was coming from amid a racket of pans and dishes.

"But I'm burning up!"

For a few seconds Miriam stood there with her arms crossed, looking at the end of the hose but when the water still didn't come out, she turned back to the railing, irritated.

"Did you shut off the faucet?"

The mother came out of the kitchen, drying her hands on her apron. "I told you I did!"

"But up here there's nothing coming out."

"Then there must not be any water pressure."

In her little hopping steps, Miriam went back and forth between the hose and the handrail, and I tried to imagine how tasty her tits would be smeared with custard.

"But look here!"

"There's no faucet turned on down here, child! If there's no water up there it's because there's no pressure! Come down and get a pailful from here."

"But the sun's going to disappear on me."

I had an itch to run my tongue over the soles of her feet until they cooled off, and then to move up her body like a rocket.

"Do it the best you can. I've got a lot to do, and the story's about to start."

The mother went back in, discussion ended.

"Mama, I'm burning!"

In a few minutes we heard the sound of the television being turned on.

"Mama, do something!"

In response, Miriam's mother turned up the volume. A sickly voice was singing, *"Rock and glass, that's what our love is made of..."*

"Why don't you come over to our house?"

Miriam looked at me surprised, like she had forgotten I was there, draped over the wall.

"Why should I come over there?"

The way she asked made me smile; it was enough to make me want to respond with something provocative, but things had gone so badly for me the night before when I was acting up that it seemed best to play it safe.

"Because over here," and I swear I said this without implying anything, "the Pelopincho is full."

When I pulled at her bikini strap at the end of the afternoon, Miriam's tits seemed like two of the most beautiful things God had put on this earth. Of course, the fact that I hadn't had a fuck for so long had a lot to do with that. But I was so hot, so needy for kissing and screwing that I couldn't think much about it then. "Finally, a woman!" I kept repeating this inwardly, congratulating myself. "Finally some loving!" Her nipples got hard when I kissed them, and even though Miriam asked me softly to let go of her, I realized from the way her skin got goose bumps that she didn't really want me to do that. And she was the one who pulled down my bathing suit. When she grabbed my cock with both hands, I confess, I nearly fainted. I licked at her body like a cat and even got my head under water to kiss her between the legs; and when neither of us could stand it anymore, I put it in her and started humping. My old lady came out of the kitchen shouting; she wanted to know what was going on, water was coming down onto the patio. I told her that one of the patches on the Pelopincho was leaking, just don't worry, and I'll fix it right away. Miriam turned around, holding on to the rim of the wading pool, and looked back over her shoulder; she asked me to please put it in again. I didn't wait. The noise of our bodies thrashing around in the water, the slapping of her ass bouncing again and again off my legs made me think of the ducks in the zoo rushing over to the edge when someone held out a bag of little crackers: thousands of wings beating frantically in a desperate race to get there first.

7

· · · · · · · · · ·

"We've been going over a lot of things with Ulysses, talking about this whole affair, and so…"

Pa didn't know how to continue.

"And so?" Miriam's father challenged him, his elbows on the table. My old man had to wipe his moustache with a handkerchief to be able to go on.

"The truth is that Ulysses doesn't want to get married to Miriam. That is the truth."

Armando, Miriam's father, is a massive guy. His hair is cut short, his eyebrows are broad, and his gut is overwhelming, hiding his belt. But no one can say he's fat. While he was listening to Pa, the muscles right under his ears got as tense as a steel cable.

"He likes her a lot," Pa went on, "but he's still young, he wants to go to school…and you know what it takes to maintain a family…Ulysses is still a little boy…"

"And so what do you think, don Mario? That my daughter is old enough to be a mother? Why is she alone the one to bear all the blame?"

Every time Miriam's father spoke, my old man looked to one side, or else he kept folding and unfolding the kerchief he dried his moustache with.

"They're both to blame," her mother interrupted.

"They have to get married!" her father insisted.

"You know perfectly well what we believe in, don Mario," Luisa's shrill voice was unbearable. "We are practicing apostolic Catholics!"

Armando pointed at me with his finger.

"As long as Ulysses has done what he's done, he's got to accept the consequences."

"My son didn't do anything to anybody." My old man opened out his arms as if saying mass. "What they did they did together!"

"Well, whatever," Miriam's mother was not going to be stopped by any argument. "We're facing an irreversible process. Miriam is pregnant, she's got a child growing in her belly and that's a lot of responsibility to share. This can be resolved in only one way."

My old man was in a corner. If my mother had been there, she would have helped defend me, but at that very moment she was lying down, lamenting in Greek, while Jorgelina was putting compresses of cool water and vinegar on her forehead.

"Why don't we just follow things as they develop?"

For the first time that evening, Armando managed to get Pa to look him in the eye, but only for a few seconds, because afterward, Pa stood up and pounded the table with his fists.

"Because they don't love each other! And if they don't love each other things will turn out bad later on!"

I never thought he would be able to react in that way, and even less so when facing an orangutan like Miriam's father, who, not to be out-done, stood up on his side of the table and also started pounding on it.

"What do you mean, they don't love each other?" he shouted. "Don't love each other! You think they would've done what they did if they didn't love each other?"

Miriam's mother also got to her feet. "I don't know what you're trying to tell us, don Mario."

"They don't love each other enough to be married, that's what I'm trying to tell you."

I'd gone over to where Miriam was. I took her by the hand and led her out to the patio. I shut the door to the living room and took her toward a corner where we could talk quietly.

"Why didn't you tell me before that you were pregnant?"

"Since we'd had a fight..."

Miriam walked over to the stairs that went up to the rooftop ter-race and sat down on one of the steps. Luisa had said, at one time early in the conversation, that she hadn't been feeling well lately.

"How long have you known?"

"Two months."

I leaned back against the wall. I couldn't stop thinking about my bad luck. Some stars were shining brightly up in the sky. Wasn't there some way to get there?

"Are you happy?" Miriam's voice brought me back to earth again.

"Happy about what?"

"That we're going to have a baby."

Miriam was so anxious for me to say yes that I wanted to smash her. How could she not realize how absurd this whole situation was?

"You're not happy?"

Miriam lived on another planet. I took a deep breath and looked down, searching for the gentlest way to say it.

"No, Miriam. I'm not happy, not at all."

It was painful to be so cruel to her; she'd really stuck with me and I'd been infatuated with her during the few months the relationship lasted, but I had to find some way to make her see how things were.

"Right now we're supposed to be in love with each other just because you're going to have a baby?" She turned away from me. "We weren't even on speaking terms…"

My sister came out to the patio with a pail of water and a bottle of vinegar. All kinds of weeping and curses in Greek were coming from Mama's room. After Jorgelina went into the kitchen and closed the door, Miriam looked me in the eye. But she couldn't speak to me; she had to lower her gaze to do so.

"When we were together I liked being with you."

"And so did I, Miriam," I was trying to be nice. "But what's that got to do with it? We already said that."

"And what has what we were saying got to do with what I'm asking you?" She raised her voice and looked straight at me with those dark eyes so full of tears that I felt like somebody had suddenly pulled the rug out from under me. "The only thing I want to know, the only thing I want you to answer is whether you want to have it."

Miriam was so sincere, her feelings so obvious, that I was beginning to feel like a royal son of a bitch.

"We'd be dying of hunger if we got married!"

"I am not going to have an abortion."

"No?"

"You don't know me, Ulysses, if you think that I am going to kill my son." Miriam had what it takes to go through walls. "He's already kicking me."

"What do you mean, kicking you?"

"I feel him moving inside there."

I looked at her belly. She was hardly showing. I suddenly got emotional over the thought that something we'd made together was growing there.

"At night, when I'm quiet, he starts moving and kicking me with his little feet." Miriam started talking like a baby. "Hi, Mommy…Hi, Ulysses…Where are you? I want to get to know you…"

Suddenly I wanted to touch her belly. Miriam sensed it because, without a word, she took my hand and put it underneath her blouse, I shut my eyes. For a minute I was a giant encircling the ocean with my hands. Something transported me to the Moon, and from there I looked down on the Earth: a gigantic, blue ball with millions of white clouds moving sluggishly around and fleeting stars cleaving space without a sound. My son, with a face just like mine, floating in space, was trying to transmit messages to me in Morse code. When I opened my eyes again, Miriam was gazing at me happily. On the stairs, leaning against the handrail with a sentimental look on their faces, cornering me so as not to leave me any way out, Luisa and Armando were also observing me in silence. Further back Pa was shaking his head resignedly.

"Look at them…You still think they don't love each other?" Armando was smiling victoriously.

I wanted to take my hands away but Miriam squeezed them tightly to her. This had all been a trick.

"Now the only thing we have to discuss is the date of the wedding and how we're going to split up the cost," Armando had moved over toward my old man and was now clapping him on the shoulder. "And it can't be very far off because we're not going to be deprived of seeing Miriam walk into the church dressed in white."

8

· · · · · · · · · ·

Three months later we were married. We rented a small two-room apartment in one of those monotonous-looking, gray apartment buildings on Avenida Panamericana, and I started working in a little neighborhood bar called the Acropolis—owned by my father—to be able to support my new family.

The Acropolis is located on the station platform in the northern part of Buenos Aires, an area which had known its most splendorous period years before in the fifties. The area really grew during those years, creating a main street where all kinds of businesses clustered. But the recessions that followed, the crises, the miraculous economic reforms that the different governments and dictatorships imposed on the country gradually ruined the small businessmen little by little until they pretty much disappeared. The few that had managed to survive saw their final hour approaching with the opening of shopping centers and huge supermarkets. The railways greatly reduced their service because so many trains weren't necessary anymore, and the Acropolis, together with the few businesses that remained, were falling into decay, a pale shadow of what they used to be. There was some activity around the lunch hour, when the workers at a building under construction nearby would come in to drink a few glasses of wine or buy some coldcuts—something that Pa decided to start selling to increase his income.

My schedule was ten consecutive hours a day, seven days a week, but I always stayed longer because it was so boring to go home and face my wife. She wanted to call the baby Cristina if it was girl, or Armando if it was a boy, and that topic kept her busy twenty-four hours a day. As far as I was concerned, on the other hand, I couldn't care less about what she was thinking. Ever since we got married I lived constantly with the feeling that my life was going down the drain, like those ships built for great ocean crossings that when they are thrown into the water suddenly founder in an explosion of bubbles because of some small mistake in the plans. I would see my image reflected in the glass of the shopwindows and I couldn't keep from asking myself the same old question, hundreds of times: Where, at exactly what moment, at which place, did I go wrong? Pa had had the Parthenon painted on the windows as a triumphal symbol of his country, but the passing of time had peeled the paint away here and there, changing that idyllic, gilded image into its present state of ruins. I saw myself with my blue smock reflected over the image and, really, it was difficult to accept the idea that that figure there was me. In the past few months a tuft of white hair had grown out on my left temple, pale as could be, and when I smelled my hands they stank like bleach.

Detached from it all, Pa would chat with customers leaning on the bar. With the passing of time, my father had gradually started getting to be like those marginal characters who were his customers, the majority of them drunk and unemployed. In actuality, they were his only friends, the only human beings he could share his memories with.

I'd watch him bent over the counter, his shoulders drooping, and I couldn't stop the feeling of misery shooting through me. My father's hair was completely white, although the snapshot that commemorated the Acropolis's opening day showed him looking a lot different. His hair used to be black in those glorious days, and his back straight. He was toasting with my mother, raising a glass, challenging the whole world from his post beside the bar. Later on, as time went by, surely the same thing had happened to him that was happening to me now. Totally bored, with nothing interesting to do or say, and with that tuft of white hair expanding imperceptibly like a plague that keeps on spreading until it takes over everything...

"At this time of the year in my village, that was in Greece, the mountains are covered with flowers, all kinds of flowers, all colors..."

The customer was a typical wino, somebody who belonged to this suburban night, his nose somewhat reddish, eyes lost in a wineglass, a few hairs plastered with hair cream over his temples, and a shirt that was weary from having gone around with him all these years.

"What was the name of your village?" When he came across two syllables together, his tongue got tied in a knot.

"Kupiás is its name," my old man responded. "Kupiás."

The wino nodded like he understood perfectly.

"Kúpias!" he repeated, trying to imitate Pa's accent but putting the stress in the wrong place.

My old man shook his head in dismay. He had the whole night ahead of him, and when he talked about the place he was born in, it seemed as if he too were smashed.

"No, no. Kúpias, no...Kupiás!" The bleary-eyed customer looked aside. There was still a tricky knot there, but this time it was in his brain. "The stress is on the *a*, not on the *u*, don't you see." My old man explained it like a lesson. "Kupiás!"

"Kupiás?"

This time he'd hit the mark. Pa clapped him on the shoulder, satisfied, and the wino, raising his hand, showed him the empty glass, his little finger held out. Pa poured another, to the brim.

"Green, yellow, red...all colors! And colors that don't even exist! You see a flower there, and you say, 'What color IS that flower?' and you don't know! Because they are unusual colors, you understand. Colors that don't exist, that don't even have names!"

I would get home with the final take for the night, and when I got to the bedroom, I almost never found Miriam awake. I realized she had tried to wait up for me because she always had a magazine in her hand, or there was a book that had fallen beside the bed, and the bedside light was on. I would cover her with a blanket so she wouldn't get cold. Since her belly had started growing out she would say she could hardly breathe and went around all day with the windows open. She would leave me a plate of food in the kitchen, and a beer in the fridge. I would stay up late watching television with my mind completely blank, and often I would wake up with the first rays of the sun coming in through the living room window. I turned off the TV and got into bed a few hours before Miriam woke up and got breakfast for me. That morning, as usual, our conversation revolved around the only topic she could think about.

"When I told Mama that if it's a girl we're going to name her Cristina she put on such a face...She could almost kill me! She's so jealous! Since if it's a boy we're going to name him Armando like my father, she wants us to name her Luisa if it's a girl. But I don't like Luisa!"

She took the kettle off the stove and came over to the table, her slippers shuffling.

"Do you like that name?"

"Which one, love?"

"Luisa, Ulysses! What do you think we were talking about?"

"Yeah, I like it."

Miriam went on talking without a letup and I lowered my eyes. With nothing else to do, I kept looking at the cup where Miriam was pouring the water to fix me my *cafe con leche*. On the surface, on top of the white foam, some grains of dehydrated coffee were floating. No matter how hard I pushed them down in the cup with my spoon or how frantically I stirred it, even if I succeeded in making a whirlpool, they would not dissolve. Somewhere I had read that when the human race is extinguished, cockroaches are going to be the only living things able to survive. But from what I could tell, the coffee grains were stronger. No cockroach had ever resisted the suction of a whirlpool in the sink. For a few seconds I imagined a world dominated by grains of dehydrated coffee. And with human beings floating in cups or piled up by the millions in jars, waiting in the supermarket carts for their turn to be consumed!

"You're nuts, Uli!" Miriam pulled me out of my reverie by shaking my arm. "Why did you throw the coffee out?"

At some point I had gotten up from the table and now was standing next to the sink with the jar of instant coffee nearly empty in my hand. The rest was going around in the whirlpool, coloring the water dark brown that was sucking it down.

9

. . . .

The day had passed, dragging itself sluggishly along, and now night-time had arrived with all its visitors. The wino was in his place again, stoically suffering through Pa's stories with the hope of snagging a free glass of wine. In the loneliness of the station platform, the voice of the old man remembering what his village was like, repeating over and over again the same anecdotes, made me feel more and more like I was living in a nightmare.

"You put your hand in any river around there, and it refreshes you completely…your head, body, everything! And just your hand, you see what I mean? Around here how much water do you have to drink before your thirst goes away? And it doesn't go away, because the water is different!"

If I kept on having to listen I would go crazy. My five senses, especially my hearing, shut out everything around me in order to concentrate solely on a drop of water that was falling from the tip of the faucet down onto a pile of dirty dishes. Drops fell one after the other, describing a clear outline through the grime, and the sound they made as they fell resounded in my head more intensely with each drop. I was lost. I didn't know if what I heard was the blood moving through my veins, the drop falling on the pile of dishes, or pistol shots that some madman was firing at a blank, imaginary target located in the very center of my brain.

"Are you okay?"

I looked over at the place where the voice was coming from, but for a few seconds everything was still in a jumble.

"For ten minutes I've been calling you from the station platform here in front. Didn't you hear me?"

Alejandro was holding me by the arm as if I were about to fall over.

"Something hurting you?"

"No, no, I'm all right," I said as soon as I could see better.

"Sure?"

"My blood pressure must have gone down on me," I lied.

Alejandro was the only one of my brother's friends I still kept up with. Actually, he was one of the few who would still visit us. He'd let a little French beard grow to disguise his growing baldness, but the effect it caused was exactly the opposite: the luxurious hair all over his chin stood out in contrast with the scarcity above. When I noticed that he kept looking at me as though I were sick, I asked him the first thing that came to mind, forcing a smile.

"So how's Claudia doing?"

"Oh, she's fine," he responded, adjusting a medical bag under his arm with a professional glance. "But the one who's really in a bad way is my mother-in-law." Here he stopped and gazed at me as if not knowing how to go on. "She slipped while waxing the stairs and broke her hip."

"That's a drag!"

"Actually that's why I came to see you," he went on. "Claudia's mother lives in Rosario and she has to go take care of her until one of her aunts gets there, and since we're at the end of the month..." Alejandro coughed and stopped again, "...and we don't have a cent..."

I lent him what he needed and when we closed the Acropolis that night I went along with him to his place. Alejandro lived with his wife and daughter in a one room apartment. The only window opened out on a vertical shaft where, eight floors up, the sky could be seen through some twisted television antennas. The double bed took up half the space they had. In what remained, there was a small table with a couple of chairs, the TV, and a small high chair they had bought for María, their two-year old.

"Do you know what time I went in to start work yesterday?" Alejandro had seated María in the high chair and was feeding her baby food off a plate. "Six in the afternoon!" He was waving the spoon around like a baton. "And I was only able to get away just a couple hours ago! Twenty-four consecutive hours in that fucking hospital!"

I pointed out to him that María's mouth was open and her arms were reaching out desperately trying to snag something off the spoon, but he still didn't seem to notice.

"You know why the doctor who was going to take over for me never came?" By this time we'd had a few glasses of wine and were both a little drunk. "You know why he didn't come?"

"Why didn't he come?" I asked, following his lead.

"Because he got clobbered by an ambulance!"

"An ambulance?"

"Can you believe it?" Alejandro had stopped, working up a head of steam, and when he saw I was laughing, he started screaming in my face, just inches away. "The ambulance from the hospital! It really messed him up!"

The situation was so ridiculous that I couldn't stop laughing.

"The apes driving those things are half asleep. Since they work at another job all day long, when they pick up the ambulance later on they go out on the street and anything can happen!"

María's arm was stretched out. She couldn't reach the plate with her baby food that Alejandro had set on top of the stove.

"Look at María..." I tried to warn him, but Alejandro wouldn't stop.

"You know how much a doctor earns in the United States?" The more excited he got, the closer he got to me. "At least five thousand dollars a month. And that's for the ones just starting out." With one gulp he emptied half a glass. "At the hospital they pay me six hundred and fifty-eight. You want to tell me what I can do with six hundred and fifty-eight dollars a month, with a wife and a baby?"

He drank what he had left and sat there staring into the bottom of the glass.

"Six hundred and fifty-eight dollars!"

Suddenly his eyes clouded over. Seated on the chair, his shoulders hunched over and his jaw hanging loose, he looked like a marionette whose strings had just been snipped with a pair of scissors.

"Every time I go to pick up my salary and they hand me my little envelope, you know what I feel like? Like thirty million Argentines are sticking their fingers up my asshole. UP MY ASSHOLE, Ulysses!"

Alejandro made an up and down gesture with his finger, and I couldn't help letting out a guffaw so strong the wine spurted out of my mouth like a jet of soda pop. Luckily I turned my head just in time, and only a few drops got on María's hair.

"You know how much these baby things cost? You know how much it costs for a box of diapers that you have to throw in the garbage after two shits?"

Alejandro poured himself another glass and sent it directly down to his stomach.

"To think that she still hasn't started school yet...that's when the shit's really going to hit the fan!"

"So why do you keep having kids then if you have so many problems?"

"Because children are the joy of life, Ulysses."

To see him shut up in that foul apartment, mouthing that stupid idea, made me feel ashamed, both for him and for me. Alejandro was like a mirror in time. With hardly the slightest room for error, he was showing me what was waiting for me in a few years. I tried to hide what I felt and smiled without knowing what else to say to him.

"So what are you laughing at? I tell you truly. Children are the joy of life...I'm serious, you chickenshit!"

Alejandro staggered, lurched backward, and without realizing it shoved the dish off onto the floor, where it shattered and splashed baby food everywhere.

"What did you do, María? What did you do?" Alejandro started swearing at her, completely forgetting what he'd just been saying a minute ago. "Is that all you know how to do, pull shit like this?"

"It was you that knocked it off, asshole!" I said, trying to stop him. "What're you shouting at her like an idiot for?"

"Me?"

"Yes, you. You pushed it off with your pants."

Alejandro lifted María and started patting her on the back, but María cried so hard and opened her mouth so wide we could see down to her tonsils.

"What with Claudia being pregnant and her not letting me come close to her, I'm going out of my mind. Any little thing that happens sets me off."

"Why didn't Claudia take her along?"

"Haven't you seen what she's like?" I knew she was pregnant but I hadn't seen her for some time. "She looks like a toad. Going to explode any minute now."

Someone rang the bell. Alejandro reacted surprised and looked at the clock over the fridge. It was close to twelve.

"Who the hell could it be at this time of night?" He was in a bad mood.

When he flipped the switch on the intercom, Martín's voice resounded throughout the entire room.

"Alejandro?"

"Who's that?"

"Martín." The voice had a metallic ring. "Is Ulysses there?"

"Yeah, he's here."

"Can you tell him to come down?"

"You know what time it is?"

Alejandro made signs to let me know that Martín was crazy.

"Tell Ulysses to come down. I've got a couple of chicks here."

"What chicks?" I put in.

"Chicks?" repeated Alejandro and looked at me as though I were hiding something.

"I don't know anything about any chicks. Ask that asshole what he's talking about."

Alejandro put his mouth up close to the microphone and talked as if he were telling somebody a secret.

"You have any for me?" he asked. "Claudia went to Rosario, and I'm all alone."

10

. . . .

The first problem came up the minute Martín told him to come along. Alejandro thought María would go to sleep right away, but the snot-nosed brat resisted, screaming like a banshee. Every time Alejandro tried to put her down in bed she cried and kicked so desperately that finally he opted to take her along, so the neighbors wouldn't think he was trying to kill her.

When we got downstairs and Martín saw the baby in her father's arms, the first thing he said was, "Is this a joke?" But Alejandro, drunk as he was, insisted that she'd be going to sleep in no time and that once asleep there was nothing that could wake her up.

Finally, the four of us got into the car, María with her eyes wide open like an owl, looking around everywhere, and we started out to look for the pussy.

The second problem came up when we were on the way, just a few blocks down the street. Every time Martín and Alejandro got together, the same thing happened. Since one of them worked for the government—Martín was secretary for a congressional representative—and the other one was a city employee, they started arguing. Every single time they saw each other!

"Ever since they got in they keep saying the same old thing, but they don't do a damn thing!"

Alejandro was sitting in the back seat with María in his arms, but he was shouting as if he were out in the middle of a field somewhere.

"You think you're the only one earning chickenfeed?" Martín answered.

"I'm a doctor," shouted Alejandro. "If I damn near killed myself going to school for seven years, that was so we'd be able to live decently. Not to be earning this pittance they pay me!"

"The fact that you're only bringing in chickenfeed doesn't mean we're a complete failure. It means that we're all working to get out of this crisis! It's all this debt that the previous governments left us!"

"You always put the blame on the ones that were in before."

"If we don't all put our shoulders to the wheel, everyone in their own jobs," Martín went on, "this country will never get ahead!"

These discussions went nowhere. Both of them were trying to pen each other in to demonstrate that their own arguments had more weight, or that what they were saying was backed up by the harsh reality we all had to live through. For me it was just like seeing the same film over and over again. In the newspapers, on TV, everywhere you went you heard the same things. Empty words trying to explain what no one was able to explain, or different ways of camouflaging what everyone already knew and was so damn sick of hearing about.

"You have any idea what we owe abroad?" Martín was relentless. "You have any idea how difficult it is to pay back the foreign banks?"

"Oh, what you're saying is old stuff, we've all heard it a thousand times. That's what the military said, the Peronistas, the radicals…It's just a pile of shit!"

They went on arguing like that until Martín parked the Citroën in front of a building. Hoping to end the argument, he turned around and reached out his hand over the front seat as a sign of truce.

"Can we break it off now?"

"For now," Alejandro answered him, holding out his hand grudgingly. "I can just argue to the death with people who think like you."

I got out of the car. Between the two of them they'd worn me out. The building we were about to go into was easily more that ten stories; the façade was brick, apparently, and from the number of signs up advertising apartments for sale it seemed like it had just recently been finished.

"Is there a sauna here?" I asked, completely amazed.

"You'll see what there is, immigrant," Martín replied.

The four of us went up in the elevator and Martín pushed the button for the third floor.

"These chicks, are they any good?" Alejandro wondered.

"The best."

"I want the wildest one," said Alejandro.

Going down the corridor on the third floor, María started whining. Alejandro immediately tried to calm her down with a pacifier.

"Where is it?"

"Right here." Martín pointed to the left. "I don't know where the daycare center is."

"Enough of this crying, now, María." Alejandro was getting anxious.

"You're going in like that?" Martín asked him.

"What's the matter?" Alejandro looked at himself. His shirt was totally wrinkled, hanging out of his pants, and he had a big wine stain on one shoulder. "We'll get it fixed up in a moment."

With one hand he tucked in his shirttail, and he covered the wine stain by shifting María around to hide it.

"Don't I look like a prince now?"

"You're out of your mind," Martín answered.

"I'd like to see you with a seven-months pregnant wife, to see if you keep yourself looking neat."

Martín took out a set of keys and without knocking or ringing the bell put one in the lock. When he opened the door and pushed us inside, the first thing we saw was a rather large room practically empty. In the center there was a new table with four chairs—their backs still wrapped in plastic—and in one corner were some buckets resting on some newspapers spotted with paint.

"And what's this stuff?" asked Alejandro.

"Tomorrow the painter will pick it all up."

"Is it yours?"

"Since last week." A smile crossed Martín's face.

"Is it really yours?" Alejandro could hardly believe it. Martín nodded happily. "And the pussy?"

"What did you think, asshole? That I was going to put out the dough so you could drink the milk?" Martín couldn't stop laughing. Alejandro was so surprised he didn't know what to say. "Just jack off if you're horny."

"You're an asshole! I've got to get up at six o'clock in the morning to go to the hospital."

"Fuck you for wanting to screw around on your wife and on top of that for bringing your daughter along to watch it all, you degenerate."

"What a chickenshit!" Alejandro repeated, disappointed.

"Here," Martín said, pulling some bills out of his pocket. "Take this and go buy a copy of *Playboy*. You're disgusting."

"What a bastard!" Alejandro went on. "Asshole!"

"How many rooms does it have, you son of a bitch?" I asked Martín.

"Three," he replied, pushing me through the door that led to the bedrooms.

They were nice and roomy, with large windows that opened out over the tree tops, and the bathroom was a real bathroom, with a tub.

"How much did it cost you?"

"Enough."

Alejandro followed us in silence. In the kitchen there was room for a small table; a translucent glass screen divided it off from the washroom. A giant refrigerator, the kind with two doors, was humming away next to the kitchen. When I opened it the light struck me full in the face.

"Did it come with a fridge?" I had never bought a new apartment, nor had anyone in my family. I didn't how how they came.

"What do you mean, come with a fridge?" Martín bopped me on the head, pretending to be funny. "You immigrant, I bought that refrigerator myself!"

Alejandro wasn't laughing. Leaning against the door frame, he held María in his arms while he looked around the place, full of envy.

"You know, I'm never going to be able to buy a fridge like that."

Martín put his hand in his pocket to repeat his little joke.

"Go on, buy yourself a *Playboy* before your brain explodes from a lactic embolism. Go on," he held the bills out in the air.

But Alejandro wasn't laughing. "How much do you make, Martín?" He was very serious.

"Why do you want to know how much I make?"

"You think I'm some kind of idiot?"

"What's the matter with you?"

"What's the matter with me? The only way you could have bought this apartment is through some kind of scam."

"Are you telling me I'm a crook?"

Alejandro was right. Martín didn't earn enough to buy himself an apartment.

"Where'd you get the dough?" Alejandro sat María down in the sink and went for him. Martín backed up until he was cornered against the glass screen.

"What's going on with this asshole?" he asked me as if asking for help. When Alejandro grabbed him by the throat, I thought he was going to push him through the screen.

"Ulysses! Do something!" Martín shouted when Alejandro lifted him off the floor.

"I'm going to beat the shit out of this bastard!"

"Cut it out, now!" I tried to separate them, but Alejandro was so drunk it was like trying to tug a mule.

"I've got a daughter and a wife, and I've got the same right to live decently as he does! This son of a bitch can do it because he's got pull. And when that happens, when the ones who are well off are the only ones who can survive, this country isn't a country anymore, it's a pile of shit!"

Alejandro was crying. Screaming and crying.

"I spent seven years going to school and now, for all the good it does me, I might as well shove my degree up my ass! And if I have to go to the hospital because my asshole is bleeding, they can't bandage it because they don't have any gauze! That's the reality, not the bullshit you're trying to sell us!"

11

· · · · · · · · · ·

When I got home I went to bed right away. Miriam had left me a plate of dinner in the kitchen but the fight between Martín and Alejandro had taken away all my hunger. No matter how much I tried I couldn't get to sleep. I couldn't understand why even Martín and Alejandro had become so unbearable to me. After all, these were my friends, the ones I had shared so many of the important moments of my life with.

I got up to get some soda water; the wine had made me very thirsty. In the darkness of the apartment I sat down in front of the window in the living room. The soda bubbles tickled my throat. The light from the street came through the window. With my gaze out of focus, I saw in that glinting the light of the same lighthouse that had been shining in that night ten years ago when Vincent got into that boat to cross the river. Where would he be now? I'd never heard anything more about him. Could he still be alive? My mind started churning around and I couldn't control it. Why not do the same thing he did? I wondered. Why not row across to Uruguay, land on shore, and keep running until I disappeared forever into the heart of the world? Where neither Miriam, nor my friends, nor my family would ever know anything about me again. Like a sleepwalker I went back to the bedroom. My thoughts kept going back to the same idea, again and again: that nobody would know anything about me anymore.

In a while, I don't know exactly how much later, I was on the roof terrace at my parents' house, lifting up the damp canvas that covered the canoe like a shroud. In the darkness, I felt like one of those thieves who take advantage of the night to get into the cemeteries—a grave robber. I lifted the canoe on my shoulders and left silently, supporting the weight of it much more easily than I had thought.

The streets were deserted. The only thing to be heard was my own footsteps. My back was sweating and my arms were tingling, but the idea of disappearing from the world like a rabbit into a magician's hat led me through the streets with a strength I had never known before.

I don't know how I got to the river. It all seemed like a dream. There was barely any wind, and as far as the eye could see the river was so calm it was like a huge swimming pool. The rays of the sun, still hidden below the horizon, were beginning to color the clouds with a whole range of different shades of violet. Even though I'd walked about half a mile with the canoe on my shoulders, I felt fresh and ready for anything, like I'd just gotten out of bed.

I put the canoe into the water and jumped in. I sank the paddle in the water. The canoe slipped gently along, it was unreal, as if God had abolished the law of gravity for a few seconds and nothing had any weight at all. The fresh air of the morning flooded my lungs, filling them with energy. I felt like I could paddle for days on end, until I'd gotten away from everything and everybody.

Using all my strength I buried the paddle into the water. The coast was quickly moving further behind me, and the water dripping from the wooden paddle was splashing up on me. I took off my jacket. Nothing could hold me back. The buoys marking the channel were behind me. Without noticing at first—I only realized it when I felt the dampness embracing me like a ghost—I was in a huge fog bank, a thick vapor only a few inches above the water. I got scared and took the paddle out of the water. Through the fog there was a glimpse of the city in the distance. The first rays of the sun were lighting up the great structures of glass and metal, making them shine like pearls on a heap of treasure. I couldn't help remembering the legend about the pot of gold at the end of the rainbow. Buenos Aires from that far off was shining like a magic city, but I knew it was only an illusion.

When I started paddling again, my strength had abandoned me completely. I still hadn't left the coast, and my arms were already trembling like jello. How had Vincent done it? He even crossed over during a storm. Had he really managed to make it to the other side of the river? Or had he drowned and was now resting anonymously on the sandy bottom?

Little gusts of wind were pushing the fog around, sketching filmy shapes in the air. I was getting alarmed. But in a few moments the fog thickened and I couldn't even see the bow of the canoe. A strange sound, like a siren, was spreading through the fog. At first it was almost imperceptible, but then it got so loud it turned threatening. Despite the fact that my muscles were not responding, I put the paddle into the water again and pushed, searching for a way out. Camouflaged in the mist a great shadow came closer. No matter how hard I paddled the shadow was gaining on me and was suddenly nearly on top of me, about to swamp me completely.

A gigantic motor yacht broke majestically through the mantle of fog, its siren sounding out. It was three decks high and more than a hundred and fifty feet long. From where I was at sea level it looked like the *Titanic*. I took the paddle out of the water before the waves made by the propellers could knock it out of my hands, leaving me adrift. In a few seconds the yacht had passed right in front of my nose and was beginning to move away. I couldn't see anyone on deck. I would have sworn it was a ghost ship until a black sailor appeared on the stern. Shaking out a bag, he tossed dozens of empty beer cans into the river. The waves pushed some of them up against the canoe. I picked one out of the water. It was American, a brand I had never seen. When I looked up the boat was already gone. The last I got to see of it in the fog that quickly occupied its place was the American flag it was flying, the well-known stars and stripes that I had seen so often in the movies.

12

. . . .

"You told me white!"

"I told you, one steak, no mayonnaise, and a glass of red wine, kid."

"No, you told me white!" I insisted.

"I told you red, kid. I don't drink white!"

It was pointless to go on arguing. I exchanged the glass of white wine for a red, and then started washing the dirty dishes of a customer who'd finished eating and was now perusing the newspaper studiously; he was interested in the horses.

"Which one do you like best, sonny?" he asked me, picking at a molar with a toothpick. "Big Head or Reinoso?"

An old fellow drinking grappa with soda and lemon down at the other end was holding his glass up signalling me that it was empty. I looked around in the boxes underneath the counter but finally had to go up to the storeroom because down here there weren't any bottles of it left.

"We're out of soda!" Eduardo shouted at me the minute he saw me start up the stairs.

Eduardo had been helping Pa for more than four years. He wasn't a bad guy, but he had one obsession that irritated me: he would always point out the obvious. If I dropped a glass he would say, "You're going to drop a glass," or if a customer asked for the check he would always repeat "The check!" right afterward even though I'd heard it well enough.

In the storeroom, safe from all eyes, I put my hand in the pocket of my smock; I just had to reassure myself that what I'd been through that morning was not merely the product of my morbid imagination.

"What are you doing up there, beating your meat?"

Eduardo was beating a spoon against the railing to get me to hurry, but I ignored him. When my blind fingers touched the cold surface of the beer can I let out a sigh of relief. It was there. What I'd experienced that morning was no dream.

13

• • • • • • • • • •

Despite having gotten very little rest I was not a bit sleepy. My eyes would close on me and my shoulders ached, but no matter how much I tossed and turned, I couldn't fall asleep. I threw off the blanket and walked toward the kitchen, thinking that a glass of wine would help me get some sleep. But passing through the living room, I couldn't help putting my hand in my jacket pocket. In the half light I contemplated the empty can once more. It was simply beautiful. The sketch of an eagle with its wings outstretched occupied almost the whole surface; the feathers were done in five different shades of ochre down to an iridescent brown, and its eyes were a gilded color, almost transparent; its claws, projecting savagely before it, gave the clear impression that the eagle was about to drop down on a prey that did not appear in the picture.

If I could get on that boat all my problems would be over. In the United States, far away from Miriam and my family, a new life would begin. To escape. Disappear. Run away. Some way or other I had to manage it.

With Chris's naked torso in my arms, and my head resting on her breasts, I can do nothing else but smile when I think of everything I've gone through to get where I am.

"Ulysses?"

"What's that, my love?"

Trying to excite me, Chris runs her finger over my mouth, slowly.

"What are you thinking of?"

I was thinking about myself, ten days ago, twisting and turning half the night, alone in the dining room of my apartment, looking at that beer can as if it were a crystal ball. If God had appeared at that moment and with some magic gesture showed me my future, I wouldn't have believed it.

"Oh, nothing, Chris," I smiled. "Nothing at all."

Not only had I managed to get myself on this boat but I'd also managed to fuck the daughter of one of the richest men on the planet, and she herself, with those fleshy lips, had promised to take me to New York.

"Don't think about Frank now, we're alone, and…" I see her feverish gaze, her breast pushing closer, obliging me to kiss it, her hands running eagerly over my body, and I can't stop thinking that luck has finally come over to my side. The marriage with Miriam was an unpardonable mistake. Very little, scarcely a few centimeters more, and my life would have been completely ruined; a few millimeters more and my whole existence would have gone over the edge of a cliff, like a mule worn out by the load it carried, into a bottomless pit. Now that this fat girl had fallen in love with me, she would let herself be squeezed like a lemon as long as she could be with me.

Even though I felt proud for having achieved the impossible, the road to success hadn't been easy. The motor yacht was moored at the dock of a private yacht club. I had tried to get into the basin with my canoe, but there was a checkpoint between the two cement breakwaters where a guard was posted twenty-four hours a day and would ask you for your membership card to make sure it was up to date before letting you inside. It was the best yacht club in Buenos Aires, and the most expensive; the board of directors had set up a failsafe security system so no intruders would get in to bother any of the distinguished guests. After my first encounter with the motor yacht in the fog bank, I spent a couple of mornings in the canoe, tied up to a large buoy that marked the exit to the channel some hundred and fifty yards from the entrance to the basin. I kept watching with the hope that the security officer would leave for a few minutes so I could get in there without being seen, but they were very good at their job, and when one of them needed to go eat or go to the bathroom, he called a second one who would immediately come out and replace him. I watched them from the canoe and could see the U.S. flag fluttering from the mast on deck over the ramparts that marked the boundaries of the yacht club's precinct. If I climbed the metal framework that held the light on the buoy I could even see the bridge.

During those mornings I spent on guard, I imagined hundreds of different arguments. Over and over again, until I was tired of them, I went through a series of scenes, mentally trying out what I was going to say and do in order to get them to let me aboard the yacht. But none of them satisfied me. After two or three days of watching, I started feeling like a castaway from a shipwreck; every minute I spent floating next to the buoy with no possibility of reaching my objective reinforced the sterility of my intentions. I'd told Miriam that Pa needed me to cover for him mornings at the Acropolis, and I'd told Pa that Miriam wasn't feeling very well and I wanted to stay at home to be with her. The excuse worked for the first two days, but now I didn't know what to come up with to keep from being found out.

I was tied up to the buoy, submerged in those thoughts, when the yacht's siren, the same one that had terrified me in the fog bank, reached my ears. I swear I'm never going to forget that moment if I live a hundred years. It was a luminous Saturday morning, the wind was blowing in from the sea, and the sky was completely open. Although the minute I heard the siren I knew what it was, for a few seconds I thought it might also belong to another boat. It sounded once again and I climbed up on the buoy to see if I was right. The river was choppy and the metal structure was swaying, but I'd gotten used to getting up there without losing my balance. Over the top of the breakwater I could see the mast with the flag pulling back. The security officer at the entrance moved his little boat over to one side and the yacht sounded its siren one more time as the prow started turning toward the open river. A few seconds later the boat was through the opening in the breakwater. My only chance to escape the nightmare that my life had become was falling through my fingers. The yacht was going to pass right in front of my nose, probably for the last time, and I hadn't even been able to touch it. As usual, the craziest idea, the most unlikely, was the one that cropped up. I was lost, I was somebody moving through life by fits and starts, like the survivor of a shipwreck, and so it was as a desperate survivor that I entered into that scene.

I remember that I crossed myself and hid with the canoe behind the buoy. The yacht meanwhile was coming closer at full speed. The submerged propellers were raising foam along the sides of the hull. The bow was moving ahead, cutting the water like a cube of butter. With my face against the rusty panel but not losing sight of the boat for a moment, I sank the paddle into the water. The fast moving yacht grew in size as it came closer, and the noise of the water beating against the hull mixed in my ears with the desperate beating of my heart pushing adrenalin through my veins. The boat was a five-hundred-story building coming down on me, a floating city on the verge of crossing the buoy line. I closed my eyes and drove hard with the paddle. When I moved away from the protection of the buoy, the bow was aiming directly at the center of my canoe. It wasn't more than fifteen yards away, fourteen, thirteen…

I raised my hands to my head to protect me from the impact and asked for God's help. The yacht flung itself against the fiberglass, smashing it into a thousand bits. In less than a second I was flailing my arms around to keep afloat. The engines stopped. The yacht continued on for a few yards, impelled by inertia at the same time as it began to put about. A sailor appeared on the catwalk and tossed me a life preserver. I swam a few strokes and got it around my neck. I was soaked, the waves were tossing me back and forth, and the wind struck me full in the face, but an enormous smile of satisfaction crossed my face.

I was only the son of a Greek immigrant, but I had succeeded. With the simple act of sacrificing my canoe I had managed to halt the triumphant passage of a motor yacht valued in the millions of dollars so they could pull me out of this city of losers once and for all. I would get on board and they would lead me to my encounter with the fabulous destiny that I was certain was waiting for me somewhere on this planet.

14

· · · · · · · · ·

The engines started up again and the motor yacht backed up to where I was floating with the life preserver. The sailor lowered a wooden staircase that descended toward the water like a caterpillar. Loosening some ropes, he freed a small platform that he dropped down and spread out, making something like a landing dock. While he helped me climb out of the water, an officer, or something like that—he had gold and black decorations sewed to his chest—came running down the steps and came over to me in a fury.

"Are you crazy?" He was shaking his fist just inches in front of my face, as if he wanted to imprint it on my face right then. "Why did you do that?"

I was still a little dazed from the jolt, with my clothes dripping wet, and I didn't know if it was a good thing for me to let them find out I knew English.

"Do you speak English?"

Fed up that I wasn't saying anything, the officer grabbed the sailor by an arm and pulled him over and set him directly in front of me.

"Translate!"

"The First Officer is asking you," the sailor started in in Spanish, "why you got your canoe in the way of our boat."

He must have been from some Central American country because he spoke with a funny little lilt.

"I didn't see you," I answered. "When I came around from behind the buoy you were right there on top of me!"

"This man says…"

A new voice interrupted him from the upper deck.

"What's going on down there?"

We all looked up. A heavy man, bald and corpulent, with hands like pianos, was staring down at us with his brow furrowed. He leaned over one of the railings. He must have been more important than the other officer because he had at least twice as many stripes.

"Why have we stopped?"

He spoke in a half aggressive kind of English, a bit like Humphrey Bogart, but I understood him too.

"Who gave the order to turn off the engines?"

"He put his canoe right in our course!" the officer tried to explain to him. "He didn't give us enough time to do anything. We had to run right over him!"

The heavy man gave a leap and threw himself down the little stairway. He came down it a lot quicker than you would have thought possible for a guy with a body like his. The stairway trembled at every step, and I felt like those terrified soldiers in the foreign legion watching as the herd of elephants sent by the enemy came rushing upon them.

"You did it on purpose!" the officer followed me, shouting. "I saw him! I've got witnesses!"

Two guys and three girls who were in their early twenties appeared on one of the upper decks and stared down at me like I was some exotic butterfly underneath a magnifying glass.

"You're not going to get any compensation for this!"

With a leap the fat man skipped the last three steps and landed on the platform, rocking it off balance it as if he were a catapult. Before I could say a word, he had me by the arm and was twisting it back like a piece of rubber. With his other hand he shoved my face against the boat's hull.

"Who are you?"

The only thing I could do was howl.

"Who are you?" the Central American repeated in Spanish this time, his voice calm.

"What are you looking for?"

"What are you searching for?"

"Name, age, and political convictions!"

"Your name, age, and political ideas."

There was no more room between the fat man's hand, my head, and the metal. In a matter of seconds my jaw was going to shatter into a thousand pieces. The fat man stretched his neck around and his head appeared just inches in front of my eyes. He was moving his mouth to say something but I couldn't understand him because I was on the verge of fainting.

"Why did you put your canoe in our way?" the Central American repeated, leaning around from behind the fat man.

The Officer had stooped down to the level of the other one's armpit and now he accused me again, pointing his finger.

"I'll bet he wants compensation!"

"I didn't see you!" I finally answered them with my mouth against the hull.

"What?"

"I didn't see you," I repeated while grimacing and hoping he would let go of me.

The officer tore off his hat and beat it against his knee several times.

"He's lying!"

Another man's voice was now coming from above.

"What's going on down there?"

The fat man, the officer, and the sailor looked up. I looked up too. There was a guy up there, very well dressed, hair completely white and face bronzed, looking down at us calmly, hardly raising his eyebrows.

"Why are we not moving?"

"This guy got in our way!" the First Mate informed on me. "There was nothing we could do but run him down! He did it on purpose!"

A younger man appeared behind the one with the white hair and also looked down toward where I was. The sun reflected off his wrist watch and for a few seconds there was a glare that hid his face. Despite my position, almost like a barnacle, and the dazzle that kept me from seeing his face, there was something about his build that seemed familiar.

"What's the matter, Captain?"

The reflection disappeared and I was able to see his face. Either I was crazy or the pain was giving me hallucinations, but the guy who was standing there was none other than that son of a bitch Vincent. He was bigger, several years had gone by since the last time I'd seen him, and now he was wearing glasses. But I knew that face like the back of my hand, I couldn't be mistaken! I sucked in all the air that would fit in my lungs and let it out in a single shout.

"Vincent!"

When he heard his old nickname, he bent down surprised.

"Vincent!" I shouted again.

"Ulysses?"

Vincent pronounced my name with a weird accent.

"Yes, it's me. Ulysses!"

And it was him. The same old, beloved Vincent! The fat guy released one of my hands and I waved it as best I could in a kind of salute. The son of a bitch had come out on deck like a true miracle, as if the sky had opened and the Virgin Mary had appeared.

"You know him?"

The fat guy didn't know if he should let me go or keep trying to engrave my face into the hull.

"Yes, he's a friend of mine," Vincent replied.

Those words were music to my ears. I was his friend! Not only was he rescuing me from the fat man but he was somebody I knew already on board. Vincent was the stamp of approval I needed, the passport to my new life. I went up the stairway in big leaps, dripping with water before the surprised gaze of them all. But it didn't matter. When I got to the deck I started for Vincent with open arms. But my old friend stopped me short, seizing my wrists in the air just when I was gong to give him a hearty embrace.

"You're soaked," he said, "and I have to go back to work in a few minutes."

15

· · · · · · · · · ·

"I never wear sport clothes." Vincent was standing in front of the closet in his cabin, his back to me, and the only thing I could see was an endless row of suits. "Nevertheless I can lend you something more casual…"

"Whatever you don't need," I told him, not to put him to any trouble.

I was standing naked in the middle of the room with a towel wrapped around my waist, and the truth is I felt a little uncomfortable in the midst of all that luxury. The boat had gone out for a short run because they needed to fix something with the engine that could only be managed when it was in motion, and in a little while we were going back to port.

"I don't know who rearranges my things so that I can never find what I'm looking for," Vincent was opening and shutting his drawers in a fury.

On the lowest shelf there were at least twenty pairs of shoes; above that, in piles of four, an entire collection of brand new shirts resting in their own plastic bags. Finally, when he pulled the last door open there were the things he was looking for: a collection of robes, several pairs of silk pajamas, and sports clothes, all kinds. While he was choosing what he would lend me, I looked around the cabin. It was so nice that if you were brought there blindfolded the last thing you'd imagine would be that you were on a boat. The only thing that let you know where you were was the portholes set into the wall. In front of the bed was a dressing table loaded down with colognes and perfumes; over that was a large mirror in three sections that reflected the whole cabin. Built into one wall alongside the bed was a stereo set. In one corner was a revolving stand with a large TV and a VCR. The controls for them were built into one of the bedside stands, and at one end of the room a narrow door led to a bath with a jacuzzi. On the rose-colored carpet my wet, smelly clothes were a detail completely out of place. One sock with the a hole in the heel, it was barely a cotton rag, gave away the calamitous level of my life. When Vincent stooped down to pick out a pair of slippers, I slyly kicked over the pile of stuff, and the sock, thank God, was buried.

"These will fit you pretty well," he held out a pair of slippers that looked like they were made for an astronaut. "Here are some socks, and it seems to me these pants are about your size."

I was about to drop the towel and start getting dressed when the door opened a crack and a fat girl leaned in.

"Am I bothering?"

"By no means." Proudly, taking her by the hand as if she were a queen, Vincent pulled her in.

She was wearing a one-piece swim suit, and she was as round as a beach ball. She had one of those huge romance novels in her hand, a real tear-jerker, almost as heavy as she was; on the cover I could see a woman dressed in nineteenth-century clothes on the verge of kissing some muscular man with long hair and a bare chest; their faces were distorted by the passion that was consuming them.

"This is Ulysses, Chris," he introduced me. "He's the brother of an old friend from Argentina."

She extended her hand.

"Glad to meet you."

Naked, wrapped only in a towel, I felt like those Indians that Columbus took to the Spanish court to show to the Queen.

"This woman you see before you," Vincent went on, "is my future wife."

"Really?" Though I couldn't believe he was going to get married to that pig, I still wished them the best.

"Congratulations!"

"Thank you." The fat girl looked at me as if I were a cannibal about to take a bite out of her.

"Is it true that he was in the canoe, Frank?" she asked timidly.

"Oh, yes," my friend replied.

"And you knew each other from before?"

"From the time we were kids. We lived in the same neighborhood. You better believe it!"

In front of her Vincent spoke as if he were selling bibles: with a permanent smile on his lips while his hands waved around in the air emphasizing everything.

"It's incredible!"

"Really incredible!" Vincent put a hand on the back of her neck.

A black maid, about fifty years of age and with her straight hair pulled back in a bun, came into the cabin carrying a basket and started picking up my clothes.

"You'll have to tell me about the girlfriends he had," Chris said to me, playfully. I went along with the game.

"Jealous?"

"Over him?" She lifted her eyes and looked at Vincent scornfully. "He's not worth the trouble."

"Oh, great!" Vincent played the buffoon. "Then I can look for another sweetheart with a clear conscience."

The fat girl was unable to avoid getting worked up as she put her arms around him at the small of his back. "I'll kill you if you do anything like that!"

Chris spoke at a speed I'd never heard anyone use before. I had to memorize what she said and repeat it back to myself in my head to be able to follow the thread of the conversation.

"Then it's best if I don't tell you anything," he answered. "You'll just get angry if I tell you what I do."

The fat girl took the bait. "And if I invite you for a bite to eat?"

"That sounds better."

We all laughed.

"So, we've been a Don Juan, have we, and never even said one thing about it?" Chris chided Vincent like a school teacher.

The maid, completely oblivious to our conversation, had found my ruined socks and was shaking her head without knowing what to do. I pleaded silently that she would just go on putting everything in the basket, but she shook her head one more time and finally turned to Vincent, disconcerted.

"What do I do with this?" she was holding up my ragged sock with the tips of her fingers, as if it were a rotten fish.

"Those are Ulysses's socks," Vincent looked at me, seeking a response. "Etta can mend them for you if you don't want to throw them away."

She was looking at me as I were one of those beggars working the escalators at the metro.

"No, they're no good anymore. I must have caught them on something when the canoe came apart."

Thinking that they would identify me with those ragged socks, in this cabin that was carpeted up to the ceiling, made me feel the worst of humiliations. I tried to rise above it, to make an offhand gesture to show that I didn't care, but that turned out even worse; I almost lost my towel.

"Shall I toss them out, then?" the maid asked.

"Wash and iron everything, Etta," Vincent tried to speed things up when he noticed how uncomfortable I was. "The socks too."

So she put it all in the basket and left the room, shutting the door. I wanted to jump out through one of the portholes and swim all the way home, grab Miriam by the neck, and squeeze it until her vertebrae cracked. Never again was she going to forget to mend a sock when it had hole in it.

"While you go on talking I'm going to go change," Chris said, opening the door. "We'll see each other again, okay?"

"Of course."

Chris gave my friend one last caress and swept out the door, swaying like a carp. She sort of waved the book she was carrying. "Bye-bye."

"Your fiancée is really nice," I said to him when the door was closed.

"Oh, very nice."

"What does she do?"

"Nothing. She's Ben's daughter, the owner of this boat."

"Who's Ben?"

Vincent answered me out of a sense of duty. "Ben's my boss, the representative of a group of multinationals, all leading companies. He's here in Argentina to resolve some unforeseen problems that cropped up in some contracts."

"And you? What are you doing with a guy like that?"

"Me?"

"Yeah. How did you come to land on this boat?"

He was standing in front of the mirror and adjusting his tie. While he meticulously tried to keep his gold cufflinks from getting out of place, he answered me in the mirror.

"Let us just say that I accompany him."

"But where have you been all this time? What did you do? Did you go to school in Spain?"

"At Harvard. Business Administration. I was only in Spain a couple of months."

"You're not painting anymore?"

He laughed. "I don't even remember ever painting."

"Well, you're really on the way up there, eh?" was all that occurred to me to add.

"I am already up there," he answered, turning around and looking at me with a grin.

He'd changed so much since the last time we looked at each other that I didn't know if I should get dressed fast and leave or if it was better to wait until Vincent went out. I must have spent some time mulling it over because when Vincent did turn around to speak he spoke in a tone that was higher than usual, like somebody trying to bring an uncomfortable situation to an end.

"And you?"

"Me?"

"Do you still have the little bar?"

I wasn't ready for a question like that. While I thought about how to answer him, I saw my old man with his hair totally white, standing behind the counter in the Acropolis, and a knot came up in my throat. Vincent was going to keep quizzing me and I would have no other choice but to tell him all about the pile of shit that was my life.

"It was a nice place."

I nodded in agreement because I couldn't even open my mouth. I tried, but I couldn't look Vincent in the face. He was trying to make a good impression on me with the enthusiasm in his voice, but the effect was exactly the opposite.

"The Acropolis was what it was called, was it not?"

I looked down at the towel, at the knot in the towel. And at the bare feet that stuck out further down.

"I got married," I managed to say.

"Oh, how nice!"

"Just a little while ago. We were expecting a child." I went on despite the fact that I had sworn not to tell this to anyone, "I did it on purpose, you know!"

"Why? Couldn't you have kids at first?"

"No, I mean the canoe, I did it on purpose." There was a long silence.

"I don't understand."

"I got myself in front of the boat on purpose, so you'd run me down and have to pick me up."

"I don't understand," he repeated.

"It's a miracle that you're here! I'm expecting a baby, and I don't want it. I don't love my wife, you understand? Why would I want a baby?"

When I raised my head Vincent was staring at me puzzled.

"Look at the way you're dressed!" I grabbed him by the shoulders. "You know how long it's been since I've bought any clothes? I work all day long, and what I earn is hardly enough to eat on." Vincent's eyebrows went into an arc above his glasses. "I know that in some other country things would turn out differently. But I can't do it alone! Vincent, you've got to help me!"

I fell to my knees and grabbed him around his pantlegs. My eyes were filling with tears.

"Take me with you! I need you to take me!" Vincent started pushing my head back but I wouldn't let go. "I'll do anything, I swear! It doesn't matter, I don't care, my family, my kid…Nothing! Even if you think I'm some kind of son of a bitch!" I raised my head and looked him in the eye. "I didn't want to get married. They made me!"

A sailor knocked on the door. "Excuse me, sir." He was tall and thin, the same black sailor who threw all the beer cans into the river the other morning. Vincent pulled on my armpits until he'd gotten me up on my feet.

"What's wrong, Willy?" He was somewhat nervous.

"Mr. Ben says for you to come up, it's urgent."

"I'll be there in a minute," he said and closed the door immediately.

"I'm in bad shape, Vincent, really bad." I was walking from one side of the cabin to the other because my heart felt like it was going to burst if he stopped me. "Can't you do something to help me?"

Vincent's hand, resting on the doorframe, was trembling imperceptibly.

"What can you do?" he asked me after a long silence.

"Anything! Whatever you tell me!"

"I can't guarantee anything right now, but if you come back tomorrow perhaps I can manage something for you."

"Tomorrow?"

He opened the door as if to leave. "Tomorrow, pretty early."

I couldn't hold back; I embraced him emotionally. But Vincent pushed me off.

"Thanks, Vincent, thank you!" I followed him down the passageway like a dog.

"Go on back to the cabin!" He ordered me, fretting.

Before doing what he ordered, I bent down and kissed his hands. "I'll remember this for the rest of my life!"

16

. . . .

I'd told Miriam I was going to a friend's and that at most I'd be back around five, but when I looked at my watch the hands were pointing to seven, and I'd just now gotten off the bus. I still had to go up over the bridge that crossed the expressway and then go a couple hundred yards more to reach the building. While I was hurrying toward it, dodging the families who took over the area every weekend to fly their kites, I was wondering what the hell I could tell Miriam as an excuse for being so late. Besides one for the two hour delay, I also had to think of something to explain what I was wearing, because the clothes Vincent had were too big, and the Central American sailor had to lend me a Hawaiian shirt covered with palm leaves and some plaid pants in red, blue, and black. I didn't want to go back home dressed like a clown, but I had no other choice. When I got on the bus the other passengers stopped talking to each other for a few seconds, staring at me. The shirt had shoulder pads and the astronaut's shoes Vincent had loaned me made me at least two inches taller. I felt like one of those swishy looking types on the covers of those magazines for queers. When I finally got home and opened the door, I was surprised to find the apartment still dark. Maybe Miriam got worried about how late I was and went over to my parents' place. Or else she'd simply gone out to buy something to fix for dinner. I wanted to turn on the light to change and hide what I was wearing but when I pushed the switch nothing happened. Was the light bulb burned out? I tried jumping up and batting at the light fixture. Instead of touching it I brushed against some paper thing that was hanging down. I was squint-ing to see what it was when the room suddenly lit up like fire, and an army of shadows ran out of the kitchen.

"Happy birthday! Happy birthday!"

Miriam was walking toward me with a cake with twenty-four little candles burning on it. Behind her, like the rats following the Pied Piper of Hamlin, were my father and mother, Miriam's parents, Alejandro and Claudia, and even my sister Jorgelina with Toti.

"What a surprise!" I was dumbfounded.

My family surrounded me singing enthusiastically. But Miriam took a step forward and started reproaching me in a low voice from behind the cake.

"We've been here for two hours waiting for you!" The candle light made her seem much angrier. "You told me you'd be back by five!"

"But I just…I forgot today was my birthday, love."

And that wasn't a lie. I'd been so crazy over what was going on that I really had forgotten it.

The song came to an end and everybody clapped. I bent my head down over the cake to blow out all the candles in one breath while Miriam kept nagging at me amid the shouts of "Bravo!" "Hurray!" and the applause. "Why didn't you tell me you were going down to the river? Do I have to find everything out from your mother?"

The whole group of guests surrounded me to offer congratulations and someone turned on the light. Miriam had to quiet down and stop nagging. The paper thing that I'd noticed was a streamer hanging from the light fixture—"HAPPY BIRTHDAY, ULYSSES"—and the ceiling was covered with paper garlands and colored balloons. But I would have preferred not to be faced with all that. Miriam was so shocked to see how I was dressed that I thought she was going to drop the cake.

"Those clothes!" Her jaw fell.

Claudia, now eight months pregnant and carrying María in her arms, was the one who ended up ruining it all. "What a pretty shirt!" she said, giving me a kiss and aiming the compliment toward Miriam. "Did she give it to you?"

My wife's forehead wrinkled up like a prune.

"No!" she screamed. "I never saw it before. Or the pants and the shoes, either!"

"Are you feeling all right, child?" Luisa asked, stretching her neck.

"Ulysses lied to me, Mama." Her eyes began to fill with tears.

"What do you mean, lied to you?"

"It's all a misunderstanding," I tried to explain, but Miriam, unable to contain herself, ran into the kitchen and slammed the door. Some candles fell to the floor, dotting it with bits of red wax, and suddenly there was a deep silence. They all looked at me expecting me to do something, but I was paralyzed. My old man sat down on a chair and clutched his head. Like everyone else, he was wearing a cardboard hat decorated with pieces of colored paper, but the rubber band holding it on had come loose and the little hat had fallen forward and now covered half his face.

"I knew from the beginning that things were going to turn out badly," Miriam's mother picked up her purse to leave, but Armando stopped her.

"Where're you going?"

"This is shameful, Armando! He doesn't even realize that we're waiting for him to go console his wife!"

Armando fixed me with a glare. Ma took a handkerchief out of her sleeve and went into the bathroom. From the kitchen came Miriam's intermittent sobbing and from the bathroom Mama's curses in Greek. Luisa, Armando, even my friends Alejandro and Claudia were staring at me as if I were the only one at fault when in reality they were the ones dragging me into this life of shit. I wanted to send them all to bloody hell. Or better, to pick up a bottle, break it on the table top, and stick it in her father's throat until he bled to death. But it was absurd to think about massacring anyone. I started picking up the candles that had been knocked on the floor and that brought me closer to the kitchen door. The only sound in the living room was my own footsteps and the noise Toti made crunching potato chips.

"You'd go right on eating in front of a dead body, wouldn't you, Toti?"

He turned bright red and my sister, embarrassed, took the chips out of his hand. In the kitchen Miriam didn't even want to look at me. She was crying and running her finger over the spoon she'd used to whip the cream for the cake icing.

"If you don't love me, just tell me, but don't make me look like an idiot! Everyone waiting here to surprise you, and your mama suddenly tells me you've been down at the river…!"

Miriam threw the spoon into the sink so hard that Claudia and Alejandro came to the doorway to see if anything bad had happened.

"Just leave us alone for a few minutes."

They disappeared, and I went over to Miriam.

"Your mother's more important than I am. You're not telling me what you're doing."

"I didn't want to say anything because Ma was there," I said to her in a confidential tone, "but I'm wearing this stuff because some asshole on the river in a motorboat didn't see me and ran into me."

She turned around, staring at me, concerned. She rubbed her eye with her hand without noticing that she was getting herself smeared with cream.

"What do you mean, ran into you?"

"A boat," I went on, putting on my most pitiful face. "I was coming out from behind a buoy and the bastards didn't see me..."

"And then?"

"They ran into me! What more do you want me to say?"

She opened her eyes up as big as saucers.

"And knocked you into the water?"

"What the hell, they sank the canoe! They cut off the motor then and threw me a life preserver. And since I was completely wet they lent me these things so I wouldn't catch cold."

Miriam threw her arms around me.

"Uli, do you realize you're just crazy?" The tears rolling down her face and neck were getting my shirt wet. "You could've gotten yourself killed!"

Her belly with our child inside pushed hard against my stomach.

"What got into you to go out there in the canoe."

"I just needed a little exercise, love. I've been getting fat since I started working in the bar all day long."

Alejandro and Claudia appeared once more and, seeing us with our arms around each other this time, they spread the news. Claudia said things were all right now, and someone put on some music. In a few minutes they came back with a pitcher of sangría.

"Hey, is it true you're going to name it Luisa if it's a girl?" Alejandro asked.

"We're still working on that," Miriam answered, drying her tears.

"Can we tell you what we think?" Claudia asked, massaging her own belly.

"Of course, you're not our best friends for nothing."

"Well, even if it's your mother's name," Claudia said, "and don't be offended now by what I'm gong to say, Miriam. To us it seems an awful mistake."

"It's just that it sounds like a name for an old woman," Alejandro put in, half-closing the door. "You've got to think of something more up to date."

"Didn't we agree that we were going to name her Cristina?" I asked.

"Miriam told Claudia the other day that it was going to be Luisa," Alejandro shot back.

"You said that?"

"That was the other day," Miriam looked at me and smiled in a funny way, as if she had a secret, "but with the surprise I've got for you today, you're not going to have any more problems with the names."

"What do you mean, no more problems?" I insisted ingenuously. "We'd said we would name her Cristina, and now you tell me it's going to be Luisa!"

"Just so there won't be any problem we'll used both Luisa and Cristina," she interrupted me with a smile.

"Luisa Cristina Stavropulos! She's going to jump out the window when she realizes what her name is!"

"No, stupid! It's not going to be Luisa Cristina. They're going to be named Luisa AND Cristina!"

"What do you mean, *they*?"

Miriam grabbed my face with both hands and gave me a kiss crazy with happiness. "It's going to be *they* because they're going to be twins!"

Miriam's parents, my parents, and even Jorgelina with Toti—working on the potato chips again—were standing in the doorway, looking like hens waiting for their ration of chicken feed.

"What a surprise, eh?" They were applauding.

"Congratulations!"

Someone put a glass of sangría in my hand and I just tossed it down at one gulp. Miriam was embracing me happily, and Toti, with a camera in his hand, was shooting off flash pictures from every corner.

"Twins?" I kept repeating, incredulous.

While they were all congratulating me and clapping me on the back, I was thinking, more convinced than ever, that God himself had sent me my old friend Vincent and the boat just when I needed them most.

17
· · · · · · · · ·

After everyone left we went to bed. Miriam was so tired she went right to sleep, but I couldn't shut an eye the whole night. The possibility of getting away on the boat with Vincent had me so superexcited that I didn't think I would ever fall asleep again. Even though I'd had more than twenty glasses of sangría, I kept turning this way and that, and I tried closing my eyes to get some rest but the only thing I could manage was to keep thinking faster and faster. That's the way it was all night. Miriam was sprawled all over the bed beside me and I had to hold myself back from hitting her on the belly with something hard. When the clock said six I got up wet with sweat, smelling like wine, and went into the shower. All those liters of sangría hadn't gotten me drunk, but my face was as swollen as if I'd been boxing for thirteen straight rounds. The cold water struck my face like thousands of needles falling from an airplane, but at least the swelling went down. When I got out of the shower and started dressing, Miriam sat up and looked at me sleepily.

"Is it twelve already?" she asked.

I looked at my watch, it was seven fifteen. "A little after twelve, love."

"I feel like I haven't slept at all," she said, yawning.

"It's just that you worked so hard yesterday." I covered her with the blanket and gave her a kiss. "Why don't you sleep a little more?"

Miriam huddled beneath the covers as if she were cold.

"Are you leaving so soon?"

"Pa asked me to come in early," I lied. "The races are on today."

Half an hour later I was walking along the pier. The cool morning air was racing among the masts of the sailboats and waking me up little by little. The sun rising over the river struck me full in the eyes and I had to put my hand up to my brow to be able to see anything besides spots. A black limousine passed me going pretty fast and with a screech of its tires on the pavement came to a stop next to the gangplank. Immediately Vincent and the fat girl's father were on deck, followed by a tall, slender woman. She had all the appearances of a secretary, wearing dark glasses and a wine-colored, tailored outfit. Despite the severe cut of the suit, you could imagine a spectacular body underneath those clothes. The chauffeur waited with the door open until Ben and the secretary got settled in the back seat and only then did he open the front door for Vincent to get in. At that moment I stepped forward and signaled him.

"Vincent!"

When he saw me he pulled a long face, whispered something to the chauffeur, and then came over to me clearing his throat uncomfortably.

"Get on board and ask for Marco," he told me in a low voice.

"Marco?"

Vincent nodded.

"What do I tell him?"

"Nothing. He already knows you're coming."

The whirring of the car window descending made him turn toward the limo.

"Always behind, Frank!" shouted the fat girl's father, pointing to his wrist watch.

Vincent ran over to the limo and Ben disappeared again behind the tinted glass. They started off. I remained alone. But I couldn't complain. To start off the first day of my glorious twenty-fifth year with a gift like this was something that didn't happen every day.

18

. . . .

The only living soul on deck was the black sailor I'd seen from the canoe throwing the beer cans into the river, the one Vincent called Willy. When I asked him where I could find Marco, he looked at me like he didn't understand. I had to repeat the question, this time much slower. Through the door that he showed me was a companionway going down, getting narrower and narrower the further down it went. The gleaming wood that lined the walls of the upper decks changed to a cheap lining of wallpaper with huge flowers and ended up as peeling gray paint over metal walls. On the final stretch it was only wide enough for one person and I had to move very carefully so as not to break my neck because the spot was practically in the dark. A sticky, suffocatingly foul smell wafted up from below. I turned into the last section by feeling along the walls. A weak glow began working its way toward me a few steps further down, and beyond that point the walls actually took on some shape, due to the light. I bent my head down to get through a small door and then I was on what appeared to be the landing of a short length of stairway that ended in the galley. One small light bulb, stained by thousands of specks of flyshit, gave off a feeble, yellowish light over the wooden work table. Something was fiercely boiling on the galley stove. Dense columns of rising steam coated a collection of pots and pans. The portholes were so covered with grease that you could hardly guess it was daytime outside. Behind the open door of what seemed to be a cold-storage locker was the cook, dressed in white with a black cap and a black mustache, who was trying, with obvious effort, to lift something heavy. Sometimes his face would be visible and moments later it would disappear.

"Are you Marco?"

"Don't talk to me, kid. Not now!"

"I'm in no hurry."

"Not now, kid! Not now!"

I kept quiet. The man went on tugging at something I couldn't see, his face was getting red, and drops of perspiration rolled down his cheeks.

"Just a second. I'll be through," he managed to snort.

"I've got time. No problem."

"A problem is the last thing you'll be for me, my friend!"

A pair of women's legs pushed out of the refrigerator and wrapped themselves around the cook like a bow around his waist.

"Hold on, baby!" he clutched at the refrigerator door and started shoving his ass back and forth, snorting like a buffalo. "Oh mama!" he shouted. "Poor little mama!"

When he was finished he stood there motionless, breathing hard as if he were on the verge of fainting, but after a few seconds he jumped back and with a brisk move of his hand jerked up the zipper on his fly.

"I'm the one you're looking for," he addressed me while wiping off his hands. Behind him a short dark woman appeared, in a maid's uniform, smoothing down her skirt. "How can I help you?"

I was about to answer when Willy, with bloodshot eyes, came up behind me and with one long finger pointed at the cook.

"You did it!"

"What are you doing here, you black son of a bitch? Who asked you down here?" Marco shouted.

"You did it again!" Willy jumped down from the landing and while he was in midair a knife appeared in his hand. "I warned you not to do that! She's my wife now!"

"Holy shit, Isabel!" The cook tried to protect himself behind the table.

"I warned you not to touch her again!"

"Willy, don't be silly! Isabel can't fall in love with anyone."

There were at least six inches of water on the floor. Marco moved to one side, splashing everything.

"You're going to pay for what you did, Marco. I'm going to cut out your guts!"

Willy leaped like a panther, landing with his whole body on top of the table. He was so long that if Marco hadn't shifted to one side he would have sunk the knife in his belly.

"Willy! My God!" Marco had torn off his cap and was beating desperately against the canned goods with it. "Isabel isn't ever going to fall in love with anybody!"

"She's my wife now!"

Willy slashes at Marco with his knife, but Marco, with surprising grace, jerks his body back and dodges it. When Willy turns to get set again, Marco bends down and grabs a frying pan from the oven. This time he stands up to his attacker. He succeeds in blocking the knife with the pan, and the shock of the metal against metal makes a shower of sparks.

"What is all this?" Etta, the maid I had seen in Vincent's room, is looking at us with a scowl. Willy, on top of the table, whines like a little boy.

"He's had Isabel again!" Willy has to bend down to keep from getting scorched by the flyspecked light bulb.

"Why did you do that, Marco?" Etta points at him as if she were a judge. "You knew Willy's in love with her."

"Go on, Etta. Everyone knows she can't be in love with anybody. The only one that idea would occur to is this fool here!"

Willy goes nuts. He almost takes off half the cook's ear with a quick swipe.

"Stop it, Willy! Stop it!" Etta screams but no one listens to her. There is nothing else she can do but wade into the water. The knife, meanwhile, strikes against the frying pan several times, and the sparks get more and more violent.

"Why do you let Marco do that to you?" Etta doesn't hold back from insulting Isabel. "Don't you love Willy?"

Willy manages to slice Marco on the cheek. But then he slips, and falls off the table onto a bag of onions. Marco, surprised, draws his hand over his face, and blood suddenly spurts from between his fingers. Enraged and not about to give Willy time to recover, he comes down on him and hits him on the head with the frying pan. This time there aren't any sparks. Just a muffled sound. Marco raises his arm to strike again but Etta, holding on to his hand, stops him. Willy gets up confused, takes a few unsteady steps, like a chicken with its head cut off, and finally collapses alongside the table, his head plunged into the water.

"My God!" Etta tries to lift him up but doesn't have the strength. "Isabel, please!"

Between the two of them they get him up and lay him out on the table. His eyes are open, and a little blood is trickling from his mouth.

"Ice!" Etta gives orders like a surgeon, but Isabel doesn't react. She can't stop staring at Willy with his open mouth. Only when Etta shoves her does she go over to the refrigerator and get some ice to pat out into a towel. Marco approaches Willy, his cheek still bleeding.

"Get out of here!" Etta shouts at him.

"And doesn't this mean anything?" he points to the slash across his cheek.

She doesn't answer. Marco, grumbling, presses a dishtowel to the wound and looks at me annoyed.

"And what are you doing here?" he asks.

"I'm Ulysses," I say, but I don't know if I should go on explaining my situation to him or get the hell out of there.

Marco smiles and holds out a friendly hand. "Frank told me all about you."

We shake hands while Etta and Isabel drag Willy's unconscious body through a swinging door. "I didn't think there would be anyone on the boat that speaks Spanish."

Marco turns around and with some indifference tosses the frying pan on top of the refrigerator. "So who'd you think you'd find down below here? Johnnies? We're all latinos down here, kid! What do you know how to do?"

"A little bit of everything."

He turns back again and slaps me on the shoulder in a friendly way. "Open a bottle of wine, then."

I go down the steps and find a rack where several bottles are. The water is up over my shoes but I make like it's nothing at all. Marco tosses me a corkscrew and I snatch it out of the air. That makes him smile. I uncork the bottle and hand it to him. The beast drinks half a liter in a single pull. Then he belches like a rocket.

"Here's to you," he says.

I don't know what to do, what to say. Marco wipes the blood off his face with the dishtowel and pours a good spurt of wine over the wound. "Wine kills everything," he says.

"Rubbing alcohol disinfects better," I offer my advice, hesitating.

He gives me a weird look, as if he didn't like anyone to correct him. "Y'know how to peel onions?"

I wouldn't have had to say yes.

"What are you waiting for, then?" he's in a foul mood. "Or are you going to spend the whole morning doing nothing? Here're the knives, in this drawer."

I start peeling. Marco scratches at his head. The wine or maybe the fight starts taking its toll because little by little his eyes go shut. I look down through my hands while they're working away, and where I should be seeing my feet I see water.

"Is a water line broken?" I ask.

Marco lifts one leg and lets out a huge fart. "It's the whole boat! And no one around here cares. We'll have to go back to Miami with this damn water!" he leans on the table. The bottle gets away from him, but Marco snags it in mid-air. "That's always the way, kid . . ."

He picks up the bottle and starts walking toward the swinging door, farting again.

"Drain stoppers! Drain stoppers! That's what we end up as. Drain stoppers!"

19

. . . .

Behind a stack of frying pans, a clock with a cracked glass face said eleven fifteen. More than three hours had gone by and I hadn't done anything but continue to peel onions. My eyes were swollen, they bulged like a frog's from all the tears, and my nose was totally swollen. Every five minutes or so, a trickle of water that I couldn't stop would fall on me, and since there was nothing else in sight, I ended up drying myself with the dishtowel that Marco had used to wipe off his blood. The cook had put a bandage over the wound and now he was sleeping sprawled out over the potato sacks. A black cat with a white ring around its eye appeared from somewhere and stared at me from the end of the table, holding out one of its paws as if I should be giving it something to eat. I stared at my red hands, stared at the cat, stared at the pail filled with onions, and I swear I didn't know what to do. When Vincent told me he could give me a job I never imagined I was going to be stuck inside a huge furnace. Dense columns of steam kept spewing out of the pot where some kind of stuff was boiling, and after three hours down there I felt nearly suffocated. Trying to get a little air I went over to the porthole that looked out on the pier. The glass, heavy with grease, had a latch that was completely rusted. I needed to breath in a little fresh air so bad that I decided to break the latch with something hard. A rolling pin was sticking out from a shelf. To make less noise I wrapped it in the dishtowel. The cat followed me around everywhere, convinced that I was getting its food ready. I stopped next to the porthole and hit the latch with all my strength. Marco jerked on his potato sacks as if the rolling pin had struck him on the head instead of hitting the latch. I didn't move. With the rolling pin in the air I waited a few seconds longer but Marco mumbled something, scratched his mustache, and went on sleeping as if nothing had happened. When I struck the second time, he shook himself again and started talking. At first I didn't understand what he was saying, but after the first few unrecognizable words, he began rubbing his prick, talking out loud.

"Suck on it, kid, suck me off!"

He was grinding his ass in his dreams as if he were fucking and every once in a while the tip of his tongue moved like a snake.

"That's so nice, baby doll, so nice…!"

The cat, attracted by Marco's move, stretched out its neck as if scenting something. Then it leaped suddenly, landing on the pile of sacks. Marco said something I didn't understand and then unzipped his pants and took out his prick.

"This is pure vitamin juice for you, pussy!"

The cat went closer, very cautious, and sniffed at it. At first wrinkling its nose as if it didn't like what it was smelling, then it reached out with the tip of its tongue and started licking it seriously. Marco twisted around like an eel on the potato socks.

"Taste it, cunt, taste it!"

If Marco were to wake up he'd be capable of busting my ass, the cat's ass, and anyone else's that crossed his path as long as he could work off his anger. I was about to get out of there to save my ass, when through the porthole I see the limo driving up, the one Vincent had set out in earlier in the morning. With a smooth turn of the wheel the chauffeur slows down and parks next to the gangplank. Vincent opens the back door and gets out of the car even before it stops. The secretary gets out after him. They are briskly walking up the gangplank and about to disappear from my view when Chris shows up on the pier and calls to him. Vincent quickly goes over to her as if to give her a kiss, but Chris shoves him away with her hand and tells him something I can't hear. But that son of a bitch Marco has started howling as if he were at an orgy. All I can see is the energy the fat girl puts into moving her hands.

"Look out, baby, look out!"

Marco waves his hands around in the air trying to do God knows what and hits the cat on the nose several times.

"One at a time, sweethearts, one at a time! That black son of a bitch's got enough for everyone!"

I beat at the latch again, and the safety lock breaks so I can finally open the window. By the side of the walkway the fat girl is complaining bitterly about something. Restrained because the chauffeur is still there, Vincent takes Chris by the arm and draws her over toward where I'm hidden. I can't resist the temptation to put my ear to the opening and listen to what they're saying.

"Don't be silly, Chris," Vincent's muffled voice reaches me.

Even though he's speaking in English now, I can't forget that night when we were walking along the breakwater with Miguel, the night

Vincent got farther and farther away in the boat until he became a barely visible dot.

"Do you think I wouldn't want to be with you?" he insists.

"If I were someone else you'd find some way to do it." Now it is Chris who is talking, still holding the huge book in her hand. "Or what were you doing with Dorothy? You were with me, with her, and on top of that you had plenty of time to do what Daddy told you to do!"

Vincent tries to take her by the hand. The fat girl dodges and shoves him off. The chauffeur, standing a few yards behind them, lowers his eyes uncomfortably.

"We always have to come back to the same thing," Vincent looks at Chris without knowing what to do. "But we already agreed that this Dorothy thing was over and done with…"

"The only thing you're interested in is my money!"

"But you know that's not true, that I love you…" Vincent was breathing hard like someone looking for reinforcements, and he comes closer to her. "Or don't you think it hurts me too when you say things like that to me?"

The fat girl looks at him in silence. The discussion is at a point where, if both sides are ready, things could still be fixed up. But when Vincent tries to hug her, Chris, in a violent and unexpected reaction, slugs him on the neck with the spine of her book.

"Are you crazy?" Vincent shouts, clutching at his aching shoulder.

"I'm not stupid, Frank!"

The gangplank above Vincent's head starts rocking, and the secretary appears.

"We're late," she says, scarcely moving her lips.

Vincent clears his throat and loosens his tie. He picks up his brief case from the ground and answers without looking at her.

"I'll be up in a minute."

Chris starts crying. She closes her fists angrily and then raises her hand, pointing at the secretary. "Do you think I don't know what's going on between you and that whore?"

The secretary opens her mouth but in the end says nothing. A white minivan is parking behind the limo. The door opens and the whole gang of Chris's friends get out. Their arms are full of packages and one is wearing a Bolivian hat. Right in front of everyone Chris throws the heavy novel in his face.

"I don't want to ever see you again!"

Then she runs up the gangplank. The secretary sees her coming and tries to get to the deck before the fat girl reaches her but it's useless. Chris runs into her like a Panzer tank. The secretary flies through the air and if she hadn't been able to hold on to the railing she'd have landed— splat!—on top of the limo. For a few seconds the only sound is that of Chris's shoes as she runs off, and the squeaking of the hinges of the gangplank still rocking from the collision. The secretary starts to get up, rubbing her heel painfully.

"Help me, Frank . . ." she finally manages to say.

But Vincent ignores her. He picks up the book from the ground and goes over it with his hand a few times trying to dust it off, to brush something dirty from it. Then he looks around and without saying anything to anybody, not even to the secretary who is still rubbing at her aching heel, goes up the boat's gangplank and is lost in the direction of the staterooms. I close the porthole window because Marco is about to come and is screaming as if somebody were trying to kill him.

"It's all for you, cunt, everything for you!"

Determined to talk to Vincent, I take off my apron and hang it on a nail. Trying not to make any noise, I get my feet out of the water and climb up the stairs while Marco, the cat settled down in his arms, dreams he's in bed with Marilyn Monroe.

20

· · · · · · · · · ·

Hidden behind one of the doors that open onto the deck and looking out through the crack between the door and the frame, I can just see Willy and the sailor from Central America unrolling a sizeable red carpet. Vincent, quite visibly nervous, watches over their work and at the same time gives directions over a cordless telephone. He's wearing a different suit than the one he had on a few minutes ago, and as he talks he runs his hand over an unruly tuft of hair several times until he gets it to stay down. Willy and the other sailor, sweating, turn around and go past the door where I'm hiding, and I practically glue myself to the metal wall. I smell the cologne Vincent has on and close my eyes, I don't know why. His voice gets louder as he comes closer to where I am, and I press myself even tighter against the door. He goes straight past me, but a little later his footsteps come back and stop in front of the door. I open my eyes. He is visible above the hinge. Leaning over the railing, giving precise orders on the phone as the wind musses up his hair, again he reminds me of those European models on magazine covers. I look down at my feet. My shoes and the lower part of my pantlegs are dripping with water. On the deck, beneath my feet, a pool; and behind me the wet tracks coming up from the galley. I try to move my fingers, but they're too numb. In the Malvinas Islands they didn't have good equipment for resisting the cold. Lots of draftees had their feet amputated because they'd gotten frozen. I think about my brother. I see him standing at the end of the pier while Vincent is disappearing on the river, intermittently lit up by the beam from the lighthouse. Then I see him stiff, pale, supported by the straps, tumbling into a grave together with other corpses. The sky is leaden gray. Some soldiers are throwing shovelfulls of earth on the bodies, others look on silently. I try to get a look at my brother's feet but the earth covers him too quickly and I can't see if he still has them or if they've been amputated. Vincent turns back, his mouth glued to the telephone, and draws near the crack between the door and its frame.

"No, no…It's confidential, absolutely confidential."

He's so deeply absorbed that he doesn't see me even though we're only a few inches apart. I'm sweating, I don't have the slightest idea why I'm hiding myself. What am I afraid of? Isn't Vincent my friend? If I hadn't raced ahead on my bicycle ten years ago to warn him they were coming to search for him, would Vincent still have his feet now? Would he be able to get the same respect and give Willy and the other sailor orders while sitting in a wheel chair? Vincent owed me a lot of things, he had to be grateful to me for being where he was. I came out of my hiding place and walked out on the deck. Vincent, leaning over the railing, is shouting instructions to a bunch of workers on the pier putting up a ring of steel barricades around the boat.

"What are you doing up above? And you're getting the carpet all wet." He's really irritated, pointing the antenna of the cordless phone at my shoes.

I quickly take off both shoes and socks, and Vincent arches his eyebrows in surprise.

"I have to talk to you—" I just get started, but Vincent doesn't give me time for anything. With a sudden move he lifts me in the air and pushes me up against the door.

"Who gave you permission to come up?"

"Nobody, but—"

"Don't you realize where you are?"

When he'd shoved me, one of my socks, fell—again those socks!—and now it looks like some dirty old thing dropped on the carpet once more.

"What I have to tell you won't take me more than a minute—" I'm trying to calm him down, but Vincent isn't listening. Totally beside himself, he tries in vain to kick my sock into the water or at least to get it off the unrolled carpet in some way. But the sock resists, it clings to the carpet's pile, and Vincent gets more and more frustrated. To help him I get down on all fours and go over to the edge of the carpet and reach for my sock, trying not to get my hand kicked in the process. I retreat in the same way and only when I'm back by the door again do I stand up. Vincent comes over to me, opening and closing his fists.

"What is the problem, Ulysses?" I realize he's making a tremendous effort to keep from sending me to hell.

"I'm very grateful for what you're doing for me, but…"

"But what?"

I know that what I'm going to tell him will make him mad, but for some reason I have to say it. "Isn't there some other place I could work?"

Vincent bites his lower lip, closes his hand up into a fist, and pulling his arm back as far as it can go, bangs on the door as hard as he can.

"Why the fucking hell did I ever pay attention to you, son of a bitch!"

"Why are you saying that?"

Vincent squats down and runs his hand over his mouth several times before giving me an answer.

"Didn't you say you'd do anything?"

"Anything, yes. But that galley is an inferno! Have you ever been down there? It'd be okay if it were just a little better. Just a little, nothing more."

"Do you think I'm going to go around bothering Ben every two minutes for a son of a bitch like you?" He looks up at me, straight into my eyes. "Listen to me," he goes on.

By the way he starts out I realize he's not about to help me. What's more, for a few seconds I have the feeling he's going to wave me goodbye. I suddenly get so nervous I start shouting at him, as if this were my last chance to stay aboard this boat.

"I'm not asking for anything much. If you talk to Ben of course something will occur to him. Tell him I helped you. That we used to be friends when we were kids."

I can't hold back. I start talking about Miguel, about everything my brother and I had done for him, about his father and my own parents, Miriam, the Acropolis, and my god! what else! Willy and the other sailor come up behind him. They look at him as if expecting an order to call the ambulance and have me taken away in a straightjacket.

"You owe your life to me, you son of a bitch!" At some point I go up to Vincent and am screaming at him just inches away from his face. "If it weren't for me you'd be rotting in the ground along with my brother! You'd be full of worms! Or a paraplegic!" I'm so upset my tongue locks up on me and I'm spitting as I shout.

I don't know how he does it, but Vincent manages to get loose and push me away from him; he gives me a slap.

"I don't owe anything to anybody!" He threatens me with the finger bearing his engagement ring. "And if you think I do, you must have misunderstood everything from the beginning! The only spot there is is in the galley, and if you don't like it you can go wherever you want. You're not doing anyone a favor sticking around here."

I pick up my socks, roll them into a ball, and put them in my shoes.

"If I gave you a hand it was out of the friendship I had with your brother and not for any other reason."

I don't even want to respond to him; if I open my mouth I'll spit at him, and if anyone hands me a knife I'll bury it in his neck and then poke his eyes out with it. So I put my shoes under my arm and, with my pants still dripping, start back down the stairs to the galley.

"You think I'm a son of a bitch, don't you?" that asshole is insistent, coming down after me as if he could make up for what he did. "You're right, if you think that. And do you want to know why?"

Next, he says something like the only way to get where he's gotten is by trampling on somebody else. But for me now, he's dead. Worse than dead. Because as I go down toward the galley, as my feet go down step by step past the cheap wallpaper, Vincent has already started to occupy that strange zone, that dark corner of the heart we all have, where our worst enemies reside: those who, at some time in the past now irrecoverable, were once on our side.

21

· · · · · · · · · ·

I had just reached the last bend in the stairway when Etta assaulted me with a shout.

"May we know where you've been hiding yourself?"

"I went up for a minute to talk with my friend."

"Can you finish coming down those stairs once and for all and get yourself over here right now?"

I took the last steps down and went toward her. The galley looked completely different. They had put bricks on the floor to hold some planks up above the water, and now everyone was walking round on those ribbons of wood, being careful not to get their shoes wet. Standing beside the table, Marco was decorating a pig that had been set up on a serving dish with its legs spread apart and a red apple stuck in its mouth. He was touching it up here and there with a cake decorator filled with some kind of cream. Meanwhile, Isabel was working alongside him, taking bottles out of the refrigerator and putting them by twos in some silver buckets filled with ice. She seemed completely indifferent to the cook, as if she'd had nothing to do with the bandage that covered a good part of his face.

"If I'm not mistaken this is about your size."

Etta unrolled a waiter's uniform hanging from a hook and tossed it over to me. I grabbed it in mid air and looked at her as if she were having her little joke. But she was so absorbed in polishing some silverware that she didn't even see me. Only when she went to take a cake out of the freezer did she see that I wasn't moving.

"How come you're just standing there like a post?" She was holding the cake in both hands, and the whole plank was rocking under her weight.

"Just what am I supposed to be doing, Etta?"

I was sure they had gotten together to put something over on me. If I put on that uniform, they were going to burst out laughing and I would look like an idiot! But Etta set the cake down and came over to me, fully into her role.

"You are going to be on one side of the table, Isabel on the other."

If this was a joke Etta was taking it a little too seriously. "When some-one on your side finishes his wine, you go over and pour. You always do it from the right. When you finish, you wipe the lip of the bottle with a napkin so no drops fall on the guest's clothing. And then, without any-one noticing that you're moving, you go back quietly to your place. Is that clear?"

The only thing I could do was say yes by nodding my head.

"I'll take care of the rest."

I measured the uniform by putting it up against my shoulders and it looked to me like it actually was my size.

"Where do I change?" I asked, still not sure what I had to do.

"In there," Etta pointed to the swinging door.

I was ready to do what she asked me when I heard what seemed like a whole squadron of motorcycles out there on the pier. Marco and Isabel stopped what they were doing immediately. Etta looked out the porthole all excited.

"They're here!" she looked like somebody announcing the death of a relative and fixed her eyes on me. "Hurry up! The uniform! Isabel, the wines!"

Isabel went up the stairs carrying the silver buckets and Etta fol-lowed with the pig on its serving dish. Despite my continuing nervous-ness, I couldn't stop myself and went over to the porthole myself to see why everyone was so changed. On the pier there were three limousines, and lots of policemen on their motorcycles were arranged around the barricades that Vincent had ordered set up earlier in the afternoon. With a ceremonious air, Ben was standing smiling on the red carpet at the foot of the gangplank, next to Vincent. When the limo's door opened and this guy with a substantial flap of flesh underneath his chin stepped out and reached to shake Ben's outstretched hand, I nearly fell on my ass. I rubbed at the glass a few times to make sure I wasn't mistaken, but there was no doubt: that bald fellow out there who was smiling and pumping Ben's hand for all it was worth was none other than our Minis-ter of Economics.

22

. . . .

A crystal lamp with small, imitation drops falls like a rain above the oak table. Wall lamps of smaller size provide a tenuous light along the sides of the room. It's a rather nice day, not humid or hot, but Etta gave orders to shut the windows and the curtains. The only sound to be heard is the gentle purring of the air conditioning keeping the air cool. The dishes prepared by Marco are being distributed with a subtle charm. The black woman has gone to such lengths that even Isabel and I seem an indispensable part of the hospitality.

"It is beyond our effective possibilities to pay so much in interest." From where I stand, the only part of the minister that I can see is his hands. Fleshy and white, they look like dead fish half-floating in the water. "For us it is practically impossible to augment that quota."

Ben, seated at the end of the table, facing the minister, speaks to the secretary in a low voice. "We understand your problems," she translates impersonally. "But you also must understand ours. The stockholders are suffering some damage due to the delay in the payments, and if this continues they will be able to put on some pressure. I believe that is not favorable either to us or to you. If it is not possible to raise the quota intended for payment of the debt, one has to effect some other compensation."

"What sort of compensation?" asks the minister.

"Well, oil, for example."

Etta moves her head imperceptibly. One of the glasses on my side is empty.

"Oil?" the minister repeats. Trying to hide his surprise, he looks to his assistant, seated beside him.

It's exasperating to find my bottle empty when I've only filled the glass half way yet. I look up to get help from the black woman but she's already seen me and now is coming over silently, pushing a cart laden with drinks. I take a step backward and very stylishly take up a bottle and uncork it.

"We would like for you to award our companies the opportunity to explore for oil in several regions," the secretary translates.

Vincent hands the minister's assistant a small, leather-covered notebook. I go to the table to finish filling the glass. The minister picks up the notebook and opens it. I spy over his shoulder. Several sheets of paper inside are covered with numbers, paragraphs marked off, and there's also a folding map of the Republic of Argentina with several areas outlined on it.

"Of course, in order for there to be a really favorable compensation for our stockholders, you would have to go along with us in agreeing to some prerogatives."

The secretary doesn't add any emphasis to her words. The minister looks up and stares at her.

"Once the exploration is under way and throughout a period of twenty years," she translates, "the price per barrel should be set at seven per cent below its international price."

"But that is impossible!"

Ben gestures for the secretary not to translate. He himself asks, though with a marked American accent, "Impossible? Are you certain that what I am proposing to you is impossible? How much is that word 'impossible' worth to you, Señor Minister?"

At three in the afternoon Ben bids goodbye to his guests, shaking hands warmly at the foot of the gangplank: the negotiations have ended very successfully. When we finished taking the dirty dishes down to the galley, my watch said it was nearly four. I had promised my father I would be at the Acropolis by this time. Besides, Miriam might well be taking a walk that way—for no particular reason, just because she felt like it—and I didn't want any of what I was planning to be found out. I knew that to keep my plan from running into any danger I had to live those next few days that remained to me as if I were several Ulysseses, as if in some way I was able to become my own double and be simultaneously on the boat, at home, and in the Acropolis. The only thing I had to manage in order to bring it off was a tight use of time, as well as a perfect mastery of the lie. I picked up my clothes and reluctantly went through the swinging door to change. Two cabins with three bunks in each one, with photos of naked women on one side, singers from Central America on the other, clad in their gaudy, shiny clothing, and a little door that led to a tiny bathroom without a shower. This was going to be my place, this was what awaited me. I changed as fast as I could, trying not to think too much about the difficult living conditions I could see ahead of me. I was ready to leave when Marco opened the door and looked at me, twirling his mustache as if he'd caught me trying to steal something.

"And where do you think you're going?"

"I have to get back to my house to finish arranging things."

"And what do you think?" he was shouting angrily while a strong smell of wine flooded the small quarters. "That the dishes have little hands and they're going to wash themselves?"

"Frank told me I could."

"Frank can go fuck himself!"

Marco went on shouting that he was the boss in the galley and I was not going to get out of there until everything was clean and as shiny as the sun and God knows what other Cuban idiocies. I had foreseen something like this and I had a twenty dollar bill in my pocket. When I put it in his hand there was no more shouting.

"You should have told me before, kid," he told me shoving me roughly through the swinging door. "God be with you, for Marco will arrange everything."

The clock on the Acropolis said ten to five when I got behind the counter.

"*The Boca, Boca, Boca team got swamped…*" I'd hardly set foot inside when that dumbbell Eduardo was already on my case singing some song about soccer. What did I care about soccer? "*…and in their own shit, those shitheads swam!*"

"Did my wife come by?"

"I didn't see her," he answered, tossing bits of napkin at my head like confetti. I brushed them off and looked around for Pa. I went to the kitchen, I knocked on the bathroom door, but no one answered.

"And the old man?"

Leaning on the counter, Eduardo was scraping the dirt out from under his fingernails with a toothpick.

"Upstairs."

That was really strange. Pa would never leave the till, not even if he was being taken prisoner.

"What happened? Is he feeling bad?" I was worried.

"He never said anything to me."

I hurried up to the storeroom. Pa had turned a case of beer on its side and was just sitting there. He looked so gloomy that for a minute I was afraid something terrible had happened.

"What's wrong, Pa?" he didn't look at me even when I went over and squatted down. "Do you feel sick?"

It was the first time in my life that I saw him with the bottom button of his shirt undone.

"*Ti ejis, patera?*" I asked him in Greek.

"Your uncle is coming," he said without moving his head off the row of cartons he was leaning against. "Your uncle from Greece."

"Taki?"

"Yes."

"And that's why you're sad?" Pa didn't answer; he kept staring at a fixed point. "How long has it been since you saw each other?"

"Twenty-nine years."

"So you're going to meet after twenty-nine years and that makes you sad?"

"What am I supposed to be happy about? This place?" he raised his arms at the storeroom full of empty boxes, the poster where you could still recognize the drawing of the Acropolis under the coats of dust, and the old bicycle they used to use for deliveries. "What have we done in all this time? Did we do anything at all? Nothing! the same old thing!"

His gaze kept getting more and more distant.

"If I'd gone to the U.S. like my brother Taki said, instead of coming here, each one of you would have a car and your own house." He closed his fists angrily and struck at his legs. "Argentina, Argentina...If I'd have gone to the U.S., like Taki told me, your brother wouldn't have died in the war!" He raised his hands to his face and started crying like a little kid. "What am I going to tell Taki? What am I going to say? I never wrote him, I never told your uncle that Miguel was killed, Ulysses...I never said anything to him."

"What was it that you didn't tell him?" I understood perfectly well what Pa was telling me, but I couldn't accept it, it was too terrible to be true.

"That your brother was killed, Ulysses...That he was killed!"

I put my arms around him. And I too; for the first time in a long time the tears rolled uncontrollably down my cheeks. I yearned to douse everything in gasoline and set fire to it. I was going to tell Pa about my plans and that we'd go to New York together, start all over again, yes, from the beginning. If Vincent objected I was going to put four bullets in his back. Him and that son of a bitch, the fat girl's father. And the Minister of Economics, I'd throw him to the sharks. If they were sons of bitches, I could be a son-of-a-bitch-and-a-half.

23

. . . .

After the news about my uncle coming, Pa hadn't felt good at all and went home. I stayed, alone. It'd been some time since the last customer had left. The clouds, fat as cows, passed single file in front of the moon. Every time some streak of lightning appeared in the sky, it reminded me of a film in which, to imitate the sound of thunder in a stage presentation, a sweaty fat guy backstage would shake a metal sheet back and forth. Is that what life is really like? Nothing more than a put-on? What is really the truth about the things that happen to us? Who do we trust? Who not? The wind, announcing that the storm would let loose any second now, started blowing through the treetops, shaking them violently. I couldn't help imagining God starting up some powerful propellers while all the angels were guffawing over that business of isobars, isotherms, and the rest of that shit they tell us about in school.

At this time of night the trains went by only once every hour, but I had no interest in going back home and finding Miriam. Standing on the edge of the station platform, I couldn't stop thinking about everything that had happened to me these past few days. The guy whose life I'd saved had thrown me over and was treating me like the last of the assholes. "Do you think I'm going to go around bothering Ben every two minutes for a sonofabitch like you?" Vincent's voice echoed in my ears like insults. Why hadn't I laced him one and knocked out three of his teeth right then and there? I was a lamebrain. A real lamebrain! The only thing that made me feel better was knowing that I wasn't the only simpleminded one. There were some who would have been even worse. What would Alejandro have thought, for example, if he'd heard what I heard in the dining room of the yacht while disguised as a waiter? What would he have said? Would he have protested? Or would he have asked them, to fork over his five per cent, no matter what it was? I felt so helpless with everything that had been happening to me that the only thing I was interested in was finding a way to screw up Vincent's life, that son of a bitch. While I was trying to come up with something, the headlight of a train appeared. It was an express, the kind that never stops here. The locomotive, with its siren blasting, brought to mind the image of the fat girl careening into the secretary. Afterward Vincent had picked up the book. On the cover were the two lovers, the woman with her eyes closed and her lips tenderly apart, and the man with his shirt in tatters, exposing his muscles and drawing closer, hoping to melt together in a kiss. But surely, to bring that about was not anything easy for them. Page after page, they would try to meet in some out-of-the-way place to declare their love for each other, but again and again the critical scene would be put off by some unexpected setback. The engineer blew his horn twice and the whole platform shook with the locomotive's deafening noise. In the midst of that earthquake I couldn't stop thinking about the fat girl and the cover of her book. How many pages did Chris have to read in order to have the satisfaction of seeing them kissing each other? The locomotive roared into the station, a raging black blur. Tons of iron were going past, within inches of my face. Could Vincent ever have fucked her really well? I imagined the fat girl's body going up in flames page after page. Her hand, like a satyr's, abandoning the book and moving slowly down toward her crotch. Chris must have had tons of those books underneath her bed. Every one of them represented the interminable nights of love that she dreamt of in her state of excitement and that Vincent would never give her. If I were to try to raise myself up to her, could I hope to be successful? The idea caused me some panic but at the same time it aroused me. I had decided to get away and leave everything behind, but…How far could I get? If the fat girl paid attention to me, would she leave Vincent because of me? Or would she use me simply as a fiery lover and squeeze the last drop out of me to win herself years of warmth and then later on break it off when the first little problem came up? What could I lose? But I was already committed. The train was rushing away from the platform. The idea of getting Vincent fucked up was beginning to grow inside me like an unhindered avalanche. Without trying to, merely by giving free rein to the images unloosed in me by the locomotive's passing, I had found Vincent's Achilles' heel. Not in the most twisted of his dreams could he imagine that I might attack him on this flank. It was a perfect idea. Now that I'd discovered it, I wasn't going to let it slip through my fingers, no way.

24

. . . .

At eight the next morning—shaved and with my whole body smelling of cologne—I am standing next to an old motor launch a hundred and fifty yards from the boat, praying that the fat girl might appear somewhere on board.

An hour later the sun is getting high. The boat shines like a pearl against the brown of the river. Willy is scrubbing the deck with a scarecrow's movements, but no sign of the fat girl.

Forty minutes later, close to ten, Willy wrings out his rags into a bucket and disappears, dragging his cleaning things after him.

At ten thirty I've worn out my nails. It's late to go down to the kitchen—where for sure Marco is going to climb all over me—and the later I start peeling onions, the later I'll be getting to the Acropolis. I don't have any time left. I start walking toward the gangplank, ready to go down to the galley and take up my slave's role when—as frail as a guided missile, as light as the steel ball on a demolition crane, as ethereal as a good platter of beefsteak smothered in French fries—my queen appears with a very sleepy face. If the boat were to tilt because of the fat girl's heft until it crashed against the pier and broke in two, I would not have been surprised. But the laws of physics seemed to want to demonstrate the exception that proves the rule, and nothing like that happened. Chris was carrying a glass of orange juice in one hand and the big, romantic novel in the other. While humanity in general ingests catastrophes and croissants for breakfast, Chris was getting sick on orgasmic sighs and orange juice.

She climbed the stairs sweating and got to the upper deck and there flung herself into one of the deck chairs. She set the orange juice glass down beside her and immediately started reading. Twenty-four seconds later I was standing in front of her. Hidden behind her book, Chris was reading intently, her fat fingers moving like tarantulas over the bodies of the characters depicted on the cover. I stood before her and stared at her with such intensity that it didn't take her long to notice my presence.

"Ulysses! Good morning!" she said in cheerful Spanish, setting the book face down on the deck so I wouldn't see it. "How's the new job going?"

"Oh, very well," I put on my best smile. "Where are your friends?"

"Sleeping."

"What lazybones!"

Chris smiled. The part of the deck where we were chatting was the solarium. There were several empty deck chairs.

"May I sit down?" I asked, pointing to one of them.

"Of course."

"What are you reading?"

"It's nothing, not important, just for entertainment."

Like someone who really doesn't give a damn, I turned the book over and paused, inspecting the cover.

"Do you like reading this sort of story?"

She tried to pretend she wasn't nervous.

"I think they're kind of amusing," she said.

"Isn't it better to live them yourself?" I congratulated myself. That was really making the best of a situation, pushing it as far as possible.

Chris hesitated. She didn't know how to go on.

"The thing is . . ." she said without finding the words. "In life the love stories are never the way they are in books," she finally added, but she was uncomfortable.

"Why not?"

"In books the people don't have any problems," she gradually came out with it. "But in life it's all so much more complicated, the stories never turn out the way you dream them."

"That's true. It's not often that things come out the way one would like…" I tried to talk with long pauses. "Most of the time one of the two ends up being a stranger to the other…" Chris followed everything I was saying, and I could tell that something was taking shape between us. "With time and the experiences that befall us in our lives, one learns that only when there is true love are things the way they are in books; it's only when one is interlinked with the other at a very intimate level that the problems disappear…" I remembered the fight I had seen through the porthole the day before and I intuited that Chris's mind was going back to relive those images. "I can say this to you because of the things that have happened to me, my own experience…"

The dart struck home, dead on. Chris lifted her orange juice as if looking for an excuse that would allow her to pretend that what she was hearing was not affecting her in the least, but she became entangled in her thoughts and started playing with the straw without deciding to bring it all the way up to her lips.

"Did I say something wrong?" I rested my hand on hers. She raised her head and looked me in the eye.

"No," she was almost stammering.

"But something is wrong," I insisted.

"It's just that what you said just now has been going around inside my head for a while now, and...I think the same as you, where there is love things are easy...but it's so difficult to be able to put it into words...with Frank, well, we do love each other, but...he has so much work to do and we have so little time together, sometimes I can't help but feel the effect of things that bother me, and . . ."

"I know exactly what you're saying."

Chris pulled up her knees as if she wanted to be alone. The message was clear. I had to get up, go away, leave her to her own problems. But that wasn't what I wanted; I needed more time with her.

"He was always like that, Chris," I added as if trying to make it seem less important.

Chris, still behind her knees, looked at me intrigued.

"Like what?"

Changing the subject seemed like a good tactic.

"Oh, a little crazy. He always tended to go overboard, in everything he ever did." Chris followed me attentively, so I decided to go on, with the first thing that came into my head. "Very likely he's got some problems in his job, and that's what makes him a little careless about other things...There was one time when he took it into his head to be a painter, and he went around all the time with an easel and his canvases slung over his back. He would spend the whole day reading books about Van Gogh, and he identified so much with what he was reading that his parents were concerned he might try to cut off one of his ears some day."

Chris looked at me completely nonplussed.

"He never told you that business with the train?"

"No"

"It's an incredible story, Chris."

"He never told me anything..."

"Well, Frank used to live very close to the train station, almost in front of it, and you could hear them all the time from his house. In those days, even at night they would go by often, and Frank started to get obsessed with them. One day, I remember, we were playing soccer in a field when a kid named Ariel came to warn us that Frank had gone nuts and that he wouldn't let a train pass. We all ran over to see what was going on."

"And then?"

"Frank had set up his easel in the space between the tracks, in front of a train just about to pull out, and he wasn't going to move for anything in the world. He said he was trying to capture the locomotive in movement. People who were on the train started sticking their heads out the windows shouting for him to get out of the way, but Frank wasn't having any of it, he didn't pay any attention to them. Standing between the rails, he was painting at top speed, putting paint on the canvas by squeezing it directly from the tubes. Finally, the engineer got down, they got into an argument, and since Frank didn't want to move out of the way, the engineer kicked over the easel. Then they started really fighting. They ended up having to give statements at the police station, and there was even a note about the whole affair in the newspaper."

"Frank did that?" Chris was looking at me skeptically.

"That, and a lot more!" I pulled my deck chair closer, ready to put the cherry on the cake. "When he was sixteen, the girls in the nieghborhood all went nuts over him, they would fight amongst themselves, and even his friends who had sisters of the same age started getting mad at him. Because he was going with several girls at once! For awhile he was with three at the same time, and two of them were sisters!" Chris looked at me, really surprised. "You can imagine that none of them ever managed to figure him out. Not even my brother Miguel knew how he did it, and he was his best friend!"

Only when I felt Chris's hand touching me to keep me from going on was I aware that I'd gone far enough.

"Can't we talk about something else?" she said.

"I'm sorry; for a moment I got carried away . . ."

"That's okay." She shook her head as if making light of the situation.

Silence. But she wanted to keep the conversation going in some way so it wouldn't be so obvious.

"Is Buenos Aires nice?" she changed the subject.

"Oh, it's very nice."

"I'd like to get to see what it's like."

"You still haven't seen it?"

"Frank and I were about to go, several times," she made a wry face, half regretfully. "But since he's always so busy, something would come up at the last minute, and . . ."

I listened to what the fat girl is saying and I swear I'm trying to hold myself back, but I can't help smiling.

"It sounds stupid, doesn't it?"

"Not at all," I tell her, trying to apologize.

"You don't have to make excuses," she interrupts me. "That's the way it is. Frank doing his thing, me doing mine." The fat girl is so sad, so dispirited, that she seems like a ball gone flat, a broken toy tossed in a garbage can.

"If you like I could show you around," I say to raise her spirits and, magic! her eyes light up.

"You'd do that for me?"

"Of course."

"You would?"

Its hard for me to believe she could get so emotional over a silly thing like that.

"You just tell me when, and I'll go with you."

"Oh, thank you!"

Etta comes out of one of the doors that open onto the deck, carrying a tray with the remains of a breakfast.

"Where have you been?" she admonishes me the moment she sees me. "Marco's been looking for you for more than an hour."

"I was right here, talking with—"

"Marco is furious with you!" she cuts me off. "I don't imagine you'll keep him waiting any longer?"

"Unfortunately, Chris, I've got to go to work now."

I get up as if to leave, putting a serious look on my face, but she doesn't take her eyes off me.

"But you haven't said anything about yourself."

"About me?"

"Yes."

For the first time I get nervous, and I smile, nonplussed.

"What do you want to know?"

"Are you in love with anyone?"

I can't believe what I'm hearing. "Why do you want to know that, Chris?"

Now Chris smiles, embarrassed, but she doesn't take her eyes off me, either. Etta keeps standing beside me, holding the tray, and I feel, for some stupid reason, that I can't lie to Chris in front of the maid.

"Can't we talk about this some other time?"

While Etta pushes me toward one of the doors with the edge of the tray, I suspect Chris wants to order the maid to leave me alone. But she only raises her book and waves good-bye with her hand. I turn around and look at her for the last time.

"I'm telling you honestly, whenever you'd like to go check out the city, you can just tell me."

25

Etta loads up the tray with a mountain of plates and dirty cups and then pushes me toward a door I'd never seen before.

"Marco's going to kill you when he sees you!"

I go down some steps with my eyes glued to the tray, where everything is rocking dangerously back and forth, trying to think up some good excuse so the Cuban won't skin me alive. I'm so absorbed in coming up with something that sounds true that when I stop to see where I am, I realize that I've come out in the passage that leads to Vincent's cabin. Either Etta made a mistake or I've gone astray somewhere. Straight ahead the passage opens into Vincent's room, but behind me it turns and seems to connect with another corridor that looks familiar. I turn around with the hope of encountering the companionway that goes down to the galley, but when I turn the corner I can't go a single step further because the Captain is blocking my way, standing there braced with his legs apart, pointing his .357 Magnum right in my face.

"Hands up!"

The cups and plates are sliding off the tray, smashing against the floor.

"Higher!"

I raise the tray a little more.

"More!"

My arms are so high my shirttail comes out of my pants. The Captain approaches without lowering his gun. I can't take my eyes off the little hole at the end of the barrel. I'm sure he's going to squeeze the trigger any minute. The captain's steps get louder and louder in my ears until they turn into the drum beats announcing my execution. I grit my teeth, expecting to feel the bullet entering my brain until it explodes, but the Captain's boots go right past me as if I didn't exist, and unexpectedly the hallway before me is empty. From what I hear, however, the same is not happening in the passage behind me. I twist my head around like a contortionist. Back there, with his arms raised as high as mine are, but a lot more afraid, is Willy, trembling like an epileptic. The Captain plants himself and puts the gun between his eyes.

"What are you doing in Frank's cabin, Willy?"

"I've never been in Mr. Frank's room at any time, sir!"

"No?"

"No, sir!"

"Then what I saw was a mirage?"

"I never went into Mr. Frank's room at any time, sir."

The Captain takes a step back and gestures to him.

"Against the wall."

Willy turns around. The Captain pushes his head downward at the same time as he kicks at his ankles, forcing him to open his legs. He appears crucified. While patting the sides of his body with one hand, with the other the Captain keeps the revolver pointed at Willy's ear.

"Turn around!"

Willy obeys. I try to watch what's going on with my head turned backward, but I can barely see beyond my raised arm plus a part of my shoulder and also the fire extinguisher hanging on the wall.

"Pockets!"

Willy shows him what he's got: a pack of cigarettes, a wrinkled kerchief, and a broken comb with a piece of mirror stuck to it with chewing gum. Since the Captain doesn't find what he's looking for he lashes out at Willy's hands, batting the things through the air.

"Shoes and socks!"

Willy rubs his fingers, painfully.

"I didn't do anything, sir!"

The Captain puts the gunbarrel up Willy's nose.

"Don't make me get the wall dirty, Willy!"

Blood comes into Willy's eyes. I remember when the Captain twisted my arm back until I howled louder than anyone had ever made me howl in my life, and I suddenly want to snatch the fire extinguisher off the wall and beat him over the head with it.

"Shoes and socks!"

For a few timeless seconds it seems as though Willy is not going to obey, but the Captain steps back a few inches and finally Willy gets down on his knees and takes off his shoes. Something about what I'm seeing doesn't fit. My eye veers toward something closer. It's there! The very thing the Captain is looking for! Flattened between the extinguisher and the flowered wallpaper is a wad of bills. If I reach out with a quick jerk while the Captain isn't looking, I can manage to snatch them and put them in my pocket.

"Your pants!"

"I swear by my mother I haven't done anything, sir!"

"I want to see your ass, Willy!" The Captain smiles cynically.

"I swear to you I'm innocent!"

The Captain cocks the gun and puts the barrell underneath his ear. The sound of Willy's Adam's apple going up and down is heard clearly in the narrowness of the corridor.

"Are you deaf? Or don't you understand what I'm telling you?" the Capitan shouts at him nervously. "I want to see your ass!"

Willy unbuttons his pants. His prick jumps out, waving back and forth like a string bean. The Captain looks at me, amused, and lets loose with a guffaw. It's clear he's not so interested in finding the money as he is in humiliating him. I'm trembling because the extinguisher is next to my head, and if he lets his eyes wander even a few inches the Captain might see the bills and put a bullet into Willy right there. Trying to win him over to my side, I smile at the Captain as if I approve of what he's doing.

"Turn around, Willy! There are two of us who want to get a look at your charms!"

Willy bends over and with both hands pulls back his cheeks. For a minute the Captain stops trying to keep his gun at the ready and stoops to the level of Willy's asshole. At that second I reach out and grab the bills without the Captain seeing me. I squeeze them tight so nothing is visible outside my hand. Willy sees what I'm doing and winks at me complicitly. The Captain looks up disappointed and then stares at me. The way he does it makes me suspect he's seen me or that in some way he sees the bills clutched in my hand. I turn my head back away from him and stretch my arms as high as I can. A little cup tips over on the tray and the *cafe con leche* slips down my neck like a snake.

"I'm going to get you, Willy. Sooner or later I'm going to get you," he threatens him, "and when I do, nigger, that's the day you're even going to insult your mother for having brought you into this world."

Afterward, and with a degree of concern I never expected, he walks over to where I am and rests his hand on my shoulder.

"Don't mess around with that piece of shit," he advises me.

The Captain disappears around the turn in the corridor, wedging his .357 Magnum underneath his belt, and Willy comes over toward me, pulling up his pants. I take the bills out of my pocket and turn them over to him. I didn't want to have any kind of problem if the Captain took it into his head to come back. I'd taken those bills as a reflex, almost unconsciously, but Willy saw it as a sign of friendship, as if for some strange reason we were in the same gang and that by doing this I was only corroborating that pact. He'd hardly finished hiding the money in his sock when he offered me a cigarette that I refused and started in to tell me the strangest of stories.

"Last year there was another sailor here, Leroy, he was black too." He talked while helping me pick up the broken plates and cups scattered over the carpet. "And Leroy and the Captain carried on like a couple of dogs, you know why? Because both of them wanted to sleep with Betsy."

"Who is Betsy?" I asked.

"Betsy used to be the cook before Marco came." He was picking up the broken pieces surprisingly fast. "Her body was so spectacular, so perfect, that it was impossible not to fall in love with her. All of us dropped like flies every time she walked by shaking her ass!"

Willy tossed what he had picked up onto the tray and took a drag off his cigarette.

"The Captain was always egging Leroy on. Every time he could he'd do something to bother him, to make Leroy look bad." The further along his story got, the more intense the color of his eyes got. "But Leroy was clever, he was quick, y'understand? He didn't let himself get caught by the Captain. He ignored him. And Betsy finally went for him, for Leroy!"

He stopped to let the smoke out of his mouth.

"In a few days, a storm cut loose on us. The waves were so high we thought we'd go down. Two days later, with one motor burned out and water in the hold, we reached Martinique."

Willy pointed the way to the galley. When we got through the door, in the semi darkness with light coming only from the one we'd just left, Willy grabbed my arm.

"But Leroy wasn't around anymore, he'd disappeared." The muscles in Willy's jaw were so tense I could only stare at him, hypnotized. "The Captain said he must have fallen overboard during the storm. But I don't swallow that, my friend. The Captain killed Leroy and threw him overboard, and in a few days he had Betsy in his cabin. And, do you know who helped kill him?"

For some strange reason I was starting to feel that the boat was a much more dangerous place than I had imagined.

"José the Panamanian!"

"José?"

I thought about that apprehensive, latino face, and the story didn't jell.

"The one from Central America?"

Willy nodded, inhaling deeply on the cigarette; his dark face was lit up with the light from the bright glow.

"Why do you think they go around together ever since that day?" Now a crazed light was in his eyes. "Before that, the Captain had no use for José, José worked in the galley, like us, he was a nobody. But two days after we got to Martinique…" Willy's hand went up toward the ceiling, pointing. "Up there!"

Up above, I thought. Where we all wanted to be.

"Night and day they go around together. José following the Captain like a dog, like his shadow. But the price is too high, my friend. That's why you're never going to see the Panamanian alone by himself. He knows the rules. With brothers of the blood these things get taken care of, he knows that the least slip…" Willy's hand drew a line across his neck like a slash. "Swaaccckkk!"

.   I swallowed hard.

"If I'd been in his shoes, Leroy would do exactly the same. They know it. And that's why they never give me any peace now. They want me to get tired of it and get out of here. But they're not going to get away with it." Blood was coming up in his eyes. "Not before I get back at them for Leroy!"

The rest of the trip we made in complete silence. Willy was smoking his cigarette and I was keeping my eyes fixed on the tray. When we reached the final stretch of companionway and appeared in the kitchen, there was Chris, obviously she had been crying. And Marco, a Marco totally different than I expected, a Marco who looked at me like someone trying to be my friend, points to me.

"There he is," he tells Chris pleasantly. "Where have you been keeping yourself?"

But Chris gives me no time to answer.

"I had another fight with Frank, Ulysses. And I don't want to be here when he gets back."

Neither Willy nor Marco—nor me either—could believe Ben's daughter had come down to the galley to look for me.

"Would it be too much trouble for you to take me today to take a look at the city?"

Chris came over toward me until she was standing close enough we could have kissed.

"Today?" I tried to disguise my eagerness.

"Yes, today," she answered anxiously, as if I were the only thing on earth capable of helping her, the only fireman able to rescue her from the flame consuming her. "Tonight!"

26

. . . .

"This is the Avenida Nueve de Julio, the widest in the world."

With Chris and her American friends in a minibus, we were heading toward Calle Corrientes.

"And these are Sarah's tits!" Doug shouted out sitting next me. "The biggest in the world!"

Doug had lifted Sarah's blouse, she wasn't wearing a bra, and now he was laughing like a hyena while she kept beating him with a plastic purse that was made to look like a folded newspaper.

"Come on, Sarah. You're not going to get mad over this are you?" Doug leaned over toward her, frowning. She wouldn't stop hitting him on the head trying to keep him away. "Give me a kiss."

Since no one seemed to be paying any attention to the scuffling, I made the most of the situation to offer my second tourist-guide's announcement of the evening.

"And that is the Obelisk," I said when we'd gone past the French Embassy and the country's penis appeared, surrounded by the lights of the heart of the city. "The tallest building in Buenos Aires," I added, even though I wasn't sure.

"Why don't we climb up?" Chris suggested, enthusiastically.

"Would it be open at this hour?" Sally asked, looking back at me from the front seat.

When we passed the Teatro Colón the driver lowered the window beside him and poked his head out.

"There's a light up there."

"Maybe we could go up."

"No, you can't go up," I said.

"Because of the hour?" Chris was intrigued.

I shook my head. "No, because it wasn't made for that."

Chris, sitting next to me, was confused. She gazed through the window. She simply couldn't believe it.

"No one goes up?"

"No."

"So, what's it used for, then?" The driver was looking at me through the rear view mirror; he was irritated, as if it were my fault.

"It's not used for anything. It's just there, it's for decoration"

Sally shook her head. She didn't understand. "In our country we don't do things without a reason."

Doug, who hadn't stopped smoking pot since we left the boat, started undoing his belt and unzipping his fly.

"I've got an obelisk too. Ya wanna see it?"

Sarah, sitting next to him, was the one who had to put up with him. "Ya wanna see it?"

"I don't believe I'm interested."

"It's a lovely obelisk. Red at the top. Ya sure ya don't wanna see it?" Doug was shouting, and he threw himself on Sarah like he was really out of his mind. "I know you're gonna like it, dear." His hand was inside his fly, and he made like he was going to bring himself off at any moment.

"The patient goes to the doctor's office and says to him, "Doctor, I've been having diarrhea for a week now. Can I take a bath?' And the doctor tells her…" But from his seat at the head of the table, Doug chokes up, he can't go on he's laughing so hard.

"What does he tell her?" Fred asked eagerly.

"He says to her…," No matter how hard he tries, the laughing keeps him from getting to the punch line.

"Doug!" Sarah gave him a good shake but it was no use. He had to hold himself up on the table and sink his head down between his arms so he wouldn't fall off his chair. "Doug! Please! You can't be so drunk that you can't even tell a joke!"

"He tells her that…" Doug made a good try, but his stifled paroxisms sent saliva flying everywhere. Finally he managed to get it out: "If you have enough you can take a bath!"

His hyena laughter exploded, infecting the whole table.

"Oh, that's so disgusting!" Sarah complained, looking like she'd bitten into a lemon.

Fred got up from his chair and went over to give Doug a high five. "That was cool, man, way cool!"

I'd taken them to a barbecue restaurant that catered to tourists. In the entryway there was a stuffed cow—everyone had their pictures taken with it, and Doug was posed kissing it on the mouth—and the walls were painted with scenes from the pampa, along with quotations from

Martín Fierro; and at the grill itself, the cooks were dressed in gaucho costumes.

"And what do ya think the most common dish in Africa is?" Doug was insistent.

"Monkey meat!" shouted Fred feverishly, getting braver at this time of night from the mixture of red wine, pot, champagne, and the glass of sherry that the restaurant served as a sort of aperitif.

"No."

"What is it then?"

Nasty disapproving looks were bombarding us like big rocks from the people at the tables next to us, but all the alcohol we'd had with the barbecue created an invisible wall that protected us, a hermetic glass enclosure that only opened to let the waiter in.

"Nothing."

While everybody else was laughing, Sarah stared blankly. I don't understand..." she said.

"Nothing, Sarah! There's nothing to eat!"

After thinking a few seconds, Sarah started laughing stupidly, hysterically, big guffaws. Fred pointed at Doug.

"That's so cool, man. Real cool!"

Chris realized I didn't understand and very tenderly rested her hand on my thigh.

"Didn't you get it?"

"No."

"The most common dish is nothing because they never have enough to eat in Africa."

I smiled, pretending she'd done me a favor.

"That's a good one."

"Doug always tells the best jokes, but sometimes they're not very nice, they're not politically correct."

I went along, even though I didn't understand what she was talking about. The table got quiet, and Chris looked into my eyes so deeply that I couldn't stop staring at her. In some way she had managed all evening to sit next to me. First in the bus, then at the movies, and finally at the restaurant. Now when she looked down embarrassed and moved her hand away from my leg because somebody had called out, "What are we going to tell Frank, Chris?" I was able to pay attention to what was going on at the table. Things were back to normal. Fred was shaking the champagne bottle and shamelessly getting Sarah all wet while at the other end of the table the waiter looked over the scene with evident disgust, and handed Doug the check. When he took out his wallet and opened it to take out the money, he suddenly stiffened at first and then he started hitting the table furiously with his closed fist.

"I can't believe it!" He was staring at his billfold in astonishment. "I can't believe it!" he said once more.

"Again?" Chris stood up in alarm.

"Four hundred dollars!" Doug held up his empty billfold as proof of the crime.

Chris quickly opened her purse and pulled out a credit card to hand the waiter. "I'll take care of it."

"But that's not the point, Chris. Someone is stealing from us."

I knew perfectly well who that was. Even though I'd had nothing to do with it—I'd only kept the money hidden so the Captain wouldn't fill Willy full of holes—I couldn't help feeling guilty.

The waiter withdrew, carrying the fat girl's credit card. Fred, with the index finger of his right hand pointing like a revolver, went over to Susan, threatening her.

"Okay, Susan, no more jokes. I want all the money on the table right now."

Fred was doing his John Wayne thing. Susan was too drunk to realize what was going on.

"All the money on the table, and don't try to pull anything on me, kid. This might be the gallows for you!"

While Fred held the tip of his finger to her temple, at that very second somebody else at a nearby table popped a bottle of champagne and the noise made Susan jump back in fright.

"I thought you really shot!" she apologized weakly as we all laughed.

"I'm really gonna shoot it off later on," Fred responded and launched himself on her, squeezing her tits in front of everybody.

The tour ended with everybody at the grill and the whole group embracing the gaucho-cooks and shouting "cheese" for the camera.

27

· · · · · · · · · ·

Doug climbs into the bow of the ship in his underpants, takes them off, and throws them into the water. The spotlight shining on him from the height of one of the masts outlines the muscles of his body, like a piece of sculpture. His lengthened, almost unreal shadow is cast as a giant on the surface of the water. Once he feels secure on the railing, he raises his arms, takes a big breath, and dives with agile grace into the void. His taut body travels slowly through the air as if the humidity and weight of the atmosphere were holding him up. These are the last days of a suffocating March, and in the heat of such an oppressive, windless night, the idea doesn't seem so crazy. Floating in the water a few yards below, the heads of Sally, Susan, and Fred follow the flight of his body. Now Doug comes up, his head breaking up the series of concentric circles that his dive had created, and then he swims over toward them with easy, athletic strokes.

Chris and I are standing on the dock a few yards from where the boat is tied up, feeling our own breath in the calm evoked by the river at three in the morning, listening to the water hit up against the rusty piles holding up the pier, and I can't help feeling that the spectacle unfolding before my eyes is completely foreign to me. Like it used to be when from inside the Acropolis in the summertime I would see the other kids on the block riding their bicycles to some swimming pool. Miguel and I had to stay behind to watch the bar because at that time of day our father would be taking his siesta. The sun's heat falling straight down over the roof of the Acropolis turned it into an oven, although from having filled in for Pa so often we were used to spending the summers like that. If for any strange reason he didn't happen to take his nap on one of those afternoons, I never, under any circumstances, would have gone with my friends, and not because I didn't get along with them. It was simply that I had seen them going off without me on so many of those hot days that if I actually had gone with them I would have felt completely out of place.

Now it's Sarah who appears naked on the railing. When she manages to get her balance, she looks down at the water somewhat afraid.

"It's very high."

The others down below sing out her name in chorus and beat the surface of the water with their hands.

"Sarah. Sarah. Sarah."

"I can't," Sarah's voice bounces off the pier and comes back turned into an echo.

"Cow!" someone shouts from the water.

Sarah holds her nose and jumps, landing in the water like a bomb. Laughter explodes.

We walked along the pier in silence. Little by little Chris has been opening her heart to me, and even though there are still some things it's difficult for her to talk about, now she is talking openly.

"I've often thought about leaving Frank. We've even reached the point of considering the possibility of not seeing each other for a period of time...But the truth is, I'm afraid to be alone, and Frank keeps himself away from me too much."

Behind us are laughter and the sounds of bodies moving in the water. I was imagining Vincent telling the fat girl he would have to be away from her, and I could imagine no less than taking my hat off to his acting abilities. Even though as far as everyone else was concerned he was putting one over on her in plain sight, Chris was head over heels in love with that son of a bitch.

"Didn't you ever know anyone else that you might have felt the same way about?"

I was trying to turn the conversation around to a place where I might tackle her myself. We'd been drinking and getting stoned (something that surprised me about her), and now we were walking slowly down the pier in the light of the moon. We went by a motorboat resting on several planks held up by barrels, and turned toward the section of the port where the cargo ships are tied up.

"There was one kid I would have liked to go out with. That was before I met Frank. He was the son of one of my father's partners. His name was Daniel."

"So?"

"Nothing...I'm so shy and it's so hard for me to talk, and I just never said anything to him."

"You mean you never even spoke to him?"

Chris shook her head, smiling self-consciously at her limitations.

"But why, Chris? Why didn't you ever say anything?"

"I don't know."

Suddenly I began to hate her. She had everything she wanted, everything a human being could desire in the whole world, and she wasn't even able to take advantage of it.

"Doesn't it seem to you that you should have said something to him?"

"I never got up the nerve…"

You could hear Doug's hyena laughter and the wanton splashing of the naked bodies in the water from afar. While I was having to put up with this fat girl and make a fool of myself, those sons of bitches were probably fucking the girls by now. What the hell did I think I was doing here with this cow? Why did I have pretend to be interested and hear all about her stupid inhibitions? I could be laughing myself to death, doing a swan dive off the ship's bow, naked, with a bottle of champagne in each hand and a red ribbon on my cock until I came up against Susan's tits. Here was Chris standing in front of me, and the only thing growing inside me was the desire to strangle her.

"What's wrong with you? Why don't you have the courage to speak up! What's wrong with you?"

My voice started getting louder. I was almost boiling over. I felt so turned off by this fat girl that I couldn't help a certain resentment filtering into everything I was saying.

"Why can't you do something, eh? Why?"

"You're looking at me in such a funny way," she was frightened.

And she was right. I felt like ripping off her blouse, pulling down her cutoffs, throwing her down over the pile of sand and gravel, and whipping her, whipping her on her butt until she was marked forever.

"What's wrong with you is that you've always had everything you wanted, that's your problem."

I turned toward her in a rage. She stepped back, afraid.

"You're looking at me so funny…"

"Funny!" I shouted hoarsely.

"Ulysses! Please!"

"This is nothing compared to what I'm going to do now! Now you're really going to see what funny is!"

Chris had turned me into that muscular, romantic hero resting on the covers of all her books, his clothes in tatters for having challenged the gods. But that person didn't exist, and what's more, if he did exist somewhere, he was never going to pay any attention to her. And someone had to explain that to her. I raised my hand as if to hit her, and Chris stooped over, covering her head.

"No, Ulysses!"

Thank God she did that! In her terrified eyes I managed to see the mistake I was about to make, and at the last second I was able to control myself.

"Chris, I love you," I said almost ashamed. "I'm going to die if you don't kiss me."

"I thought you were going to hit me in the face," she was disoriented, still rolled up in a ball.

"But why would I want to hit you…" I put my arms around her, feeling the whole warmth of her body as if I were hugging an oven. "The only thing I want is to feel your lips against mine. I know that sounds crazy. I know Frank is your future husband and my best friend. I know all that. But I can't help feeling what I feel. I can't help it."

28

You already know what happened later on. With the help of the cockroaches that I used to throw down the sink when I was a kid, complemented by my father's advice, I succeeded in pulling Chris to her first orgasm. That night we made love three times. The first time you've already heard about, the second time she licked me for hours until I came between her breasts, and the last time was a real abuse: she raped me while I was sleeping. Chris didn't have those hundreds of romantic novels under her bed I thought she had: instead it was all porno films. And books. To disguise them, the covers were all alike, because what the fat girl really devoured like bon bons, one after the other, were erotic novels, pornographic books, books about sexual techniques. And in that respect, I have to give her credit, Chris was a true virtuoso, and really horny. In matters of the bed, she knew all the tricks.

29

. . . .

The hands showed twenty after four in the morning when Chris fell asleep. Minutes earlier she had reassured me that the boat would go back to the United States in a few days and she would take me to live with her in her apartment in New York. But I can't stay here any longer, I don't want to arouse any kind of suspicion. Miriam is expecting me, and since I never went to work nor even let Pa know, there are definite possibilities for a big scene. I get dressed silently and leave the cabin with my shoes in my hand.

In the half-light of the passage, weakly lit by the security lights, several empty beer cans tossed on the carpet barely glimmer like fish just pulled from the water. Curious, I put on my shoes and keep walking, trying not to kick any of them in front of me. I don't know where Vincent is or what the hell Chris told him the last time they talked that kept him from coming back to sleep in his room, but I didn't want him to see me coming out of her cabin for anything in the world.

On the stairway that goes up to the deck there are more empty cans; I have to walk carefully to keep from kicking them. The higher up I go the more there are. I can't imagine what happened for all these cans to be here. Did Chris's friends have a party without telling us?

In the passageway that goes from one side to the other across the boat, the cans cover practically the whole floor. It's impossible to walk without pushing them in front of me. I forge ahead very carefully, trying to plant my feet into the spaces in between them, when I notice the Captain at the other end of the passage, talking to himself, completely drunk, holding a can of beer in his hand. I stand stockstill, unsure of what to do, with one foot in between the cans and the other still in mid-air. In a few seconds, the Captain senses that I'm there and levels his finger at me.

"You, come here!"

I go closer. I can't help noticing the butt of the .357 Magnum poking out of his belt.

"Ulysses, is that you?"

I nod my head. The Captain takes a couple of good swallows.

"I like that name...Ulysses...survivor of the Trojan war. Name of a hero, great soldier..." He's so drunk he can hardly keep on his feet. "Not like our presidents, they've got the power of the greatest country in the world in their hands, and they're afraid. International opinion...Shit on international opinion!"

His head is shaking nervously, and when he raises the can to his mouth, half of what pours out goes down his front, all over the decorations he's wearing on his chest. When he finishes he crumples the can as if it were made of paper and tosses it over his shoulder.

"Five atomic bombs. I personally saw them, myself. On the aircraft carrier *Mayflower.*" He gets another beer from one of his pockets. "I never understood why we didn't use them," he confesses bitterly to me.

Behind the Captain, Willy comes into view. He is picking up the cans and quickly tossing them into a big plastic bag, clearing up the deck. He looks at me. But I can't look back at him. I'm afraid of what might happen if I let my eyes wander. The Captain, oblivious to me, to Willy, to the boat, with his eyes as glassy as a splintered windshield, puts his hand on my shoulder.

"Y'ever seen a Vietnamese?"

"No."

"Y'ever hear one scream?"

"Never," I respond, and I don't know why, but I square up my shoulders like a soldier.

"They're not human...when you've got one of them stuck on the blade of your knife, screaming just inches in front of your face, y'almost feel their filthy breath while they're twisting around on their way to dying, you look at their eyes and in their eyes there is nothing...empty!...and they give a shudder as the life leaves them and...POOF! They fall on the ground like a sack of potatoes."

The Captain fixes his gaze on the ground as if the corpse were there on the deck between us, and there he stays, supporting himself on my shoulder, rocking back and forth as if he were going to crumple up any minute. Willy walks by again with his bag now full of cans—the passageway is absolutely clean—and tries to catch my eye to find out if he needs to help me in some way. The Captain, without turning me loose, his hand still squeezing my shoulder, not even lifting his head, starts shouting like a madman.

"What's wrong with all of you? You don't like working for a white man? D'ya hate for whites to order you around? Is that the problem?" he looks up. "Why is that can on the floor there, Willy?"

"I don't see any cans on deck, sir."

"You don't see anything, eh?"

"No, sir."

The Captain, without taking his eyes off him for a second, lets the can fall from his hand and roll along the deck until it hits the metal footing that supports the railing.

"And what is that thing there? A piece of shit?" He is shouting as he points to it.

Before Willy can answer, he grabs me violently by my shirt front.

"What is that thing lying there?" he asks me.

"It's an empty beer can, sir."

"An empty beer can lying on the deck, is that it?"

"Yes, sir…" I try to look at Willy to let him know I can't do anything else.

"Why does he see that and you don't, Willy? Because he's white and you're black? Is that the difference? Pick up that can and get out of here before I cut off your balls."

Willy picks it up and puts it in his sack.

"And take a shower when you finish, Willy. Like all the rest of the niggers, you smell like shit!"

30

· · · · · · · · ·

I get on the bus. The sky is starting to get light but the streetlights at the intersections are still on. At the last stop, just before the bus climbs the hill, a street hawker gets on. The driver lets him on without asking for a ticket—as if they'd known each other all their lives—and the man lifts the sheet of paper that covers the basket of churros, deep-fried the way crullers are, giving off a penetrating fragrance of something just recently taken out of the oven. He offers the driver a couple of monk's balls, a little like big doughnut holes. I can't stand the temptation and so I buy a dozen cream-filled churros and, sitting alone in the back seat, I wolf them down one after the other, the whole dozen, with the absolute conviction, confirmed with my departure a few days later, that a long time is likely to go by, maybe even years, before I ever taste anything so Argentine again.

I gaze at the streets of the neighborhood, deserted at this time of day, and I don't know if it's because I'm sensitized by my forthcoming departure, but as the bus moves along, I start to see my life again as if it were all a movie. I see the school going past where I did my first years, Filippo's bicycle shop, the ice cream shop where I used to go with my brother Miguel to eat ice cream cones dipped in chocolate. It all seems both far away and very recent at the same time, as if the buildings, the trees, and the pavement were faded images in an old movie. The bus turns down the street where my parents live and the singing of the sparrows coming down out of the branches fills me with sadness. I slide toward the other end of the empty seat to get a better look at the house where I was born, where I'd spent the greatest part of my life, when I realize that the person signalling the bus to stop is my mother. Miriam is beside her, dressed in the only garment for pregnant women we could get at a price we could afford at the second-hand American clothing boutique. She says good-bye to my mother and walks toward the bus while counting her money.

"Wait until I can help you, Mama."

"Thanks."

Taking her by the hand, the street hawker helps her get on. Miriam climbs up laboriously, her huge belly rocking, but oddly enough, despite the fact that I know I'm going to be found out, I feel calm. For a few seconds I imagine it wouldn't be such a bad thing to tell her the truth now. I could get another dozen churros, and we'd eat them together sitting in the back seat and I would tell her everything that had happened to me since the boat first crosssed my path.

The sound of the ticket when the metal teeth punched through it is what, thank God, jerks me away from those ridiculous thoughts. Because the only reality is that if Miriam discovers me, my whole plan goes up in flames. In the few seconds it takes the driver to handle the ticket, I turn my back and glue myself to the back door and ring the bell. The driver pulls a sour face because the bus is already moving but he opens the door for me.

"You should have let me know sooner, kid."

With a jump I'm out. When the bus starts off I turn and look. Miriam is making her way painstakingly down the aisle. I watch her moving away, sitting down awkwardly, and opening the window, and I think that, whether they are trying to or not, everyone and everything are separating from me: Miriam in that bus getting further and further away, my friends with their stupid arguments, my parents who didn't do a thing to help me get out of a marriage that from the beginning was bound to fail. Everyone in one way or another had made it so the only thing I could think about now was leaving.

Dragging her slippers, stooped, bathed in the orange light of dawn filtering through the trees, my mother is also moving further away. She is moving her lips as if talking to herself. She walks toward the house but I don't even try to get her attention. Instead I follow her behind the parked cars until she stops at the door and starts talking to Armando. What's everybody doing up at this hour? All this fuss because I didn't come back last night? I can't quite hear what they're saying, but the expressions on their faces are very serious. Something bad has happened. When Armando says good-bye to her in his troubled way and goes into his own house, I come out of my hiding place and run over to where she is.

"Where were you?" she asks in a broken voice, her eyes red like she hasn't slept all night long.

"What happened?"

"Your father…" she tries to talk, and collapses into my arms with her eyes filled with tears. "Your father, Ulysses!"

The pants, shirt, and undershirt Pa always wears, even in summer, I toss it all on the floor and sit down on the chair beside him. His mouth is open and his eyes are closed. With his hands resting on the bedspread, he is breathing as if something in his chest were broken. I don't know how long I stay there, staring at him. But when the light starts coming in through the cracks in the blinds and the snapshots of Miguel, Jorgelina, and myself around the crucifix start glistening in the room's half-light as the only treasures accumulated after a long life of privations, sacrifices, and hard work, I can't stand it any longer and get up.

I go out to the patio. Sitting at the kitchen table, Mama is staring fearfully into the bottom of the cup, as if she didn't have the courage to read the future in the coffee lees as she's always done because this time it has to do with her husband's life.

"What did the doctor say?"

She looks up and quickly rinses the coffee cup under the stream of water from the faucet.

"He has to sleep more, keep from losing his temper, work less…"

"What's wrong with him?"

"Your father is depressed, Ulysses…"

"Depressed?"

"He's sick…He doesn't want your uncle to come."

"Papa told you that?"

My mother doesn't answer. She senses that I know the truth about that. That Pa never sent the bad news to Greece, the mourning envelope you're supposed to send when a relative dies, the envelope he should have sent when he got the telegram from the army informing us that Miguel had been killed in the Malvinas.

"Why doesn't he want Taki to come?" I asked her again as if it were the only possible way to get rid of the guilt, the grief I'm starting to feel because I know I'm going to be abandoning them.

"Your father never says anything. Or haven't you noticed?" She clutches at the marble tabletop as if she were going to fall. "He keeps everything back. He swallows it. And you, you never realize a thing."

"Me?"

She clutches at my arm. "When are you going to realize?"

"Realize what, Mama?"

She knows that as long as I'm pretending not to know what she is talking about, I'm not doing anything but putting off the moment when I take my father's place, once and for all. That's why she looks at me so disappointed.

"When he gets home from work he can hardly walk because of his legs," she tells me, trying to make me feel some compassion.

"His legs?"

"His varicose veins, they're breaking out all the time…If you tell him not to go to the Acropolis anymore he'll listen to you, Ulysses…You he'll listen to…But you have to promise him you're going to work, that you're going to go…Or do you think the Acropolis is for your sister? You're the only one left now."

I couldn't help seeing the mess in the sink behind her. Rags to soak. Bandages spotted with blood. My father's blood, from his varicose veins.

My mother says good-bye but I can no longer distinguish where I am or what I say. The only thing I want is to go back to the boat, put a gun to the Captain's head, and force him to weigh anchor right now.

"Here are the keys." She puts the key ring my father always had hanging from his belt into my hand and forces my fingers to close over it. "I'm going to go in at noon, after the doctor comes, so you can eat something."

"All right, Mama."

She caresses me, for the first time in a long time.

"Everything's going to turn out all right," she tells me, choking up.

When my mother closes the door I stare at the keys I have in my hand, the ones my father carried around his whole life long, and in a moment of revelation I see everything clearly, as if transparent, for the first time. It was the keys' fault that Pa had to get up at six every morning. His life was ruined only because those keys existed and along with them the obligation to go through with the daily ritual of raising the metal shutter every morning and taking care of his customers. I throw the keys away and run. I run as if a pack of rabid dogs were chasing me, as if only by running that way, like escaping a plague, I would be able to leave for good everything that ties me to Buenos Aires. I run, I cross the streets, the plaza, I pass the door of the school I'd seen from the bus a few minutes earlier, and I keep on running. I go down the hill. My lungs are bursting, I can't get any air into them, but I keep on running. Not until the yacht club, the pier, and the boat appear before my eyes do I stop. A helicopter is hovering over the breakwater. It's suspended in midair, throwing its shadow over my body like a guillotine. Trying to keep it in sight, I trip over the edge of the tar and roll on the ground. The helicopter moves ahead a few yards and then, gently coming to earth, lands next to the gangplank. The metal feet hardly brush the pier when

Ben, Vincent, and the secretary appear on deck. Protecting themselves with their hands so the wind doesn't muss them up, they run over to the machine. Vincent is about to get into the plastic bubble when he recognizes me. I'm still lying on the ground, trying to weather a sharp pain in my knee, when he is upon me.

"What the hell are you looking for, asshole? To get me to kill you?" Before I can answer, Vincent grabs me by the shirt front and pulls me up. "What did you tell Chris?"

"Nothing." My face is distorted in the reflection from his glasses. "She told me you'd had a fight."

In the helicopter a bodyguard is waving a weapon.

"Chris told you that?"

"I swear it."

The bodyguard, a mastodon with dark glasses, runs toward us with a gun in his hand.

"And what did you tell her?"

I look around in my head for a reply.

"What did you tell her, son of a bitch?" Vincent screams at me impatiently.

"That I love her."

"That what?"

"If she hadn't told me first, I swear I wouldn't have told her."

He lets go of me.

"Chris told you she's in love with you?"

The bodyguard is sweating when he comes over. "Any problem?"

"Please," Vincent stops him with hardly a move. "This is a private matter." With a sign he waves him away.

"It's not the first time she's told me that…" I add when the bodyguard steps back. To make it more believable, I make the sign of the cross over my lips. Vincent takes a few seconds to recover before addressing me again.

"Did you make love?" he asks.

Although his eyes remain motionless, I know that for him every second I delay in responding means pocketsfull of dollars that Chris flings on the scale, tipping it toward my side.

"I can't answer that, Vincent." I say this knowing that all the cards are coming my way and that he can't do anything to stop me. For the first time since we've met again, his hands seem to be stuck in his pockets in a gesture of defeat.

"I know I've been careless in my relationship with Chris. But we love each other, and that's what counts. So I ask you not to see her again, Ulysses, because the only thing you'll do is confuse her..."

Ben pokes his head out of the plastic bubble, gets out of the machine, and shouts, like he always does, that they are behind schedule.

31

．．．．．．．．．．

"Chris, I know him too well. He's capable of anything!"

Smothered in the tumbled sheet she looks up at me.

"He doesn't seem to me to..."

"But don't you realize? You're Ben's daughter. While Vincent was with you, his job was secure. But now your father can throw him out any time!"

"Frank is an excellent professional."

"What's that got to do with it? Being a good professional, what difference does that make? If Vincent thinks he can lose his job, he's capable of inventing anything as long as it makes me look bad."

I can't stop, I'm like an animal in a cage, pacing from one side of the cabin to the other. On the other hand, Chris is looking at the alarm clock, rubbing its face dazedly, and when she sees what time it is she screws up her mouth in an expression of annoyance.

"Is it only nine in the morning?"

"What?"

Chris lifts the clock and shows it to me.

"Is this clock working all right?"

"I'm talking to you about something important!" You fat bitch, I'd really like to shout at her, Get up off the bed and do something!

"I never get up before eleven."

"But this is an emergency, my love."

To answer she buries her face in the pillow, irritated.

"You don't know Vincent, Chris. I know what he's capable of. I'm afraid." I sit down beside her to get her to pay attention to me.

But she has something else on her mind. Although I take her by the wrists trying to stop her, she pulls the zipper down on my fly and puts her hand in.

"Chris, are you listening to me?"

My question is meaningless because actually, she can no longer answer.

"I love you. This is the first time in my life that I've felt good with somebody," I say, caressing her hair, "and that means a lot to me."

"Where have you been all my life?" she closes her eyes, amo-rously.

"I'm talking to you about something important!"

Chris is licking my cock, running her tongue along the thickest vein, and then she brings me off by turning the palms of her hands in opposite directions.

"The only thing that matters is this…" In an outburst of erotic eagerness she squeezes me hard enough that it hurts, and then she takes my cock in her excited mouth. I'm holding tight to the bedframe, put-ting up with the wild sucking. "As long as this belongs to me, no one is going to do you any harm, Ulysses. No one."

I open my eyes. In the bathroom, Chris, reflected in the mirror, is drying her hair. I'm not sure what it is—the noise of the hair drier fills the cabin—but I think I hear someone knocking at the door. I'm looking around, hunting for the clock to find out what time of day it is, when I hear the knocking again.

"Chris…" I want to warn her that someone is out there but my voice won't come out. My mouth feels doughy. I lift my head up a few inches above the pillow. Parts of my naked body are all mixed in with the sheets. Again I hear the knocking, but this time Chris has turned off the drier and hears it too.

"Who is it?"

"It's me, Willy. I'm bringing you your breakfast."

I manage to wiggle the sheet around enough to cover me when Willy comes in, carrying a tray. He sees that she's in the bathroom and smiles at me like we're part of a conspiracy. I greet him with a smile too, but when Chris comes into the bedroom in her robe, we both get serious again. Willy asks where to put the breakfast tray and Chris's whole re-ply is a half hearted wave in the direction of the bed while she's putting perfume on the lobe of her ear. I pull in my legs to make room, and Willy sets the tray on the bed. When she goes back to the bathroom, Willy takes advantage of the moment to raise his hand to the level of his shoul-der as a kind of greeting, like I've seen in the movies. I do the same and feel like I'm already in New York; I touch his palm with mine.

"You are the best!" he tells me, showing his teeth. "The best."

Just then Chris comes back from the bathroom. She falls on the sheets, nibbling at a piece of toast, and Willy leaves with his head down pretending that we don't even know each other. Chris slides over to me if to give me a kiss. Turning into the lover, I close my eyes for a fraction of a second, and when I open them again Vincent is pushing Willy out of the room. Then he locks the door with a key and puts it in his pocket.

"This morning I told you I didn't want to see you again," he addresses me threateningly, as he gets closer, "but it seems that words don't have any effect on you."

"Frank, please!" the fat girl screams and puts herself in between us.

Vincent pushes her out of the way.

"Do I have to beat the shit out of you to make you understand?" he shouts.

I get out of the bed, covering myself with the first thing that comes to hand, and Chris slips between us again trying to calm things down. Vincent grabs her by the hair and throwing her backwards forces her head down toward the floor.

"Did you make love with him?"

"You're hurting me, Frank."

The fat girl's hand reaches out for some support to keep her from falling, but Vincent keeps on dragging her around the room.

"He's married," Vincent spits out. "Married and expecting a child."

"Please, you're hurting me."

"Ask him to take you to his house!" Chris is trying to get him to open his fist by scratching his fingers. "Did you ask him why he doesn't introduce you to his parents?"

"You always knew how to get me all mixed up," the fat girl is panting; she's hurting. "You always convinced me to do what was best for you. But this time I'm going to do what I want! Ulysses loves me like no one ever loved me in my life, and whether he's married or not I don't care!"

"How can you be so stupid?" Vincent shouts and yanks her hair even harder. Chris's eyes fill with tears.

"That's what I always was to you. Stupid! A fat girl you could do anything with. But I'm fed up with it. Fed up!"

She starts beating on his chest with her fists but he doesn't let go.

"Ulysses is a fraud. He's lying to you. He's married. He only wants your money!"

I can't hold back and start shouting at him from the other side of the bed, thinking too that (at least for my later benefit) I have to do something to defend her. "That's what *you're* after! The only thing you want is her dough, you son of a bitch!"

What happened next is a blur. Vincent and I start fighting, and suddenly, I don't know how it is, he's sitting on my stomach with his hands around my neck, squeezing hard. I try to hit him in the face, but my arms are too short. Three or four times I see my fists going up there in vain, and that's the last thing I see. After that everything seems to cloud over. I also see something bright and glowing, and Vincent is weaving around like a sheet blowing in the wind until he disappears and then I see everything white, as if I were on top of a mountain and the glare of the snow kept me from seeing whatever was around me. I hear voices, the sound of something dragging and falling, but I haven't the slightest idea where I am. Until everything goes blank.

I'm awakened by the lightbulb of the upended table lamp which is miraculously still working among the remains of the bedside table scattered over the carpet—that little lightbulb shining directly at me. The first thing I see is the knot of a necktie, then the starched shirt collar, the heavy, short hair around an ear, and blood. A trickle of blood oozing from hair-covered skin drips onto the carpet. I move back. Altogether, those distinct, separate parts form Vincent's head. I put my hand up to the back of my neck because I feel something throbbing there. Leaning against one of the walls, with her legs doubled up and arms solidly around her knees, Chris is crying silently. I struggle to get my feet and step over Vincent's body, taking care not to trample on the pieces of the nightstand lamp spread around on the carpet.

"Is it true what Frank said?" Chris asks me between sobs. "Is it true that you're married and expecting a baby?"

I put my arms around her. Her arms, broad as a buffalo's thighs, are shaking with her whimpering and her tears.

"Do you think I would be with anyone else besides my wife if I were expecting a child at any moment?"

Chris looks me in the eye. I realize that she really is confused, that she doesn't know how to answer me.

"Chris, you know me. You know I couldn't do that."

She starts crying again her head against my chest and I hug her with all my strength.

"I told you, Vincent is capable of doing anything to make me look bad."

32
· · · · · · · · ·

Between Willy and José the Panamanian, Vincent is hauled out on a stretcher. I watch them from the bed. Seconds earlier I've had to go lie down again because one of the blows Vincent gave me during our struggle, just behind the ear, occasionally makes me feel dizzy. Etta is picking up the pieces of the table lamp with the help of a broom and a dustpan. She looks at me without understanding how, by what means, from my simple post as galley helper, I've managed to get here in the bed that Vincent has occupied without interruption, at least for the last four years. Doug, Susan, Sarah, and, I think, Sally poke their heads in the door, curious. Chris, wringing a damp handkerchief, lets them know what happened to him. I keep touching the spot behind my ear, where a continual buzzing keeps punching at my eardrum. From the looks on the Americans' faces when they look at me, I realize that the news that I am Chris's new lover must be going around the boat, from mouth to mouth, hand to hand, like a stick of dynamite with the fuse lit. Etta finishes her work and goes out. Chris takes advantage of the situation to get rid of her friends and return to my side.

"Do you feel better?" she asks, running her hand over my forehead. I reply that I am.

"Everything's going to turn out all right, she says, drying her tears.

Someone knocks at the door. The Captain walks in without waiting for an invitation.

"Captain!" Chris exclaims, surprised by the sudden invasion.

"We have to talk, young lady!"

He closes the door behind him and Chris stands up, nervously adjusting her robe.

"Now?"

In the next few minutes, giddy, vague—like a coin turning wildly in the air not knowing if it's going to come up heads or tails when it lands—Chris, the spherical Chris that I have been so mean to because of her obesity, is revealed to me for what she truly is: Ben's only daughter and therefore his only heir. And for the first time since this whole story began, I understand Vincent's desperate need to hold on to her.

"Frank was choking him, that's why I hit him on the head with the first thing I picked up." Chris is trying to convince him not to report it to the police.

"I am the one in charge of security on this boat. You should have warned me first."

"But Frank was choking him."

"Frank is entitled to bring legal action against us, if he so desires."

"But I can't be blamed, it was self defense."

"It would have been self defense if he'd been hitting you."

While this was going on, José comes into the stateroom with the news that the ashtray Chris had conked Vincent on the back of the head with had made four neatly spaced holes in his scalp, but there were no further complications. This information quiets the Captain down for the moment, and he withdraws after warning me that later on he wants to have a chat with me in private. I answer that I have no problem with that, but then the buzzing turns into a drill working its way into my ear and the whole room starts whirling around me.

"In respect to the other thing," I hear the Captain saying, "the only thing he needs is his passport."

"I imagine he must have one…" I just barely hear Chris saying.

She comes over to the bed and her face appears like the full moon against a smooth sky.

"You do have a passport, Ulysses?"

"Passport?"

"For the trip. We get under way in a couple of days."

Yes, I think, the passports that Miriam and I had gotten when Armando hinted that thanks to a friend we might be able to take a honeymoon trip on a Caribbean cruise special offer. The passports. Inkstained fingers, the two by two color photo, and myself naively convinced that marriage might have its advantages after all.

"Ulysses, what's the matter with you?" Chris's voice sounds like she's in a tunnel. "Ulysses! Ulysses! Captain, get the doctor!" she screams, very far off. "Get the doctor!"

33

· · · · · · · · ·

My ear is still throbbing but the pain is bearable. The moonlight is coming in through the porthole and the glowing hands of the alarm clock on the nightstand show three twenty. The first image that comes into view is that of a stethoscope listening to my chest, then a transparent pill with little multicolored spots that someone puts on my tongue, and a glass of water. But the thing that worries me most is Chris's voice asking me for my passport.

Despite the hour—it's still dark—the bus is almost full. Workers, most of them, are going to the factories. I'm squeezed in with them, hearing the murmur of their conversations, until they all get off at once at the same stop and the bus is nearly empty. The only other passenger left is sleeping with his mouth open, sitting in the back seat, leaning up against the window. The workers cross a parking lot, headed toward a gray building with a smoking chimney. I sit down and watch them walking away. With the bus in gear and starting off, my eyes turn down to the floor. I read the newspaper headlines: "STRONG REACTIONS AGAINST ECONOMIC MEASURES." Pictures of an overturned bus, tires burning in the middle of the street, and workers being pursued by the police. "GOVERNMENT WILL NOT PERMIT BREAKDOWNS," proclaims another headline in thick letters. On the following page, a picture of the Minister of Economics. The very hand I'd seen leafing through the notebook Ben handed him is trying to deal with the swarm of microphones surrounding him. He explains that the disturbances are the work of agitators sent by the opposition. "The incidents are in no way a response to any real claims," he assures us. Two pages later, almost unnoticed, an article at the bottom of the page: "IMPORTANT ACCORDS REGARDING OIL EXPLORATION FINALIZED."

I get out of the bus and start up the metal bridge over the expressway. I stop in the middle. The structure is vibrating because of the trucks. If I were to tie the minister up around his armpits and dangle him overboard on a rope, would the trucks come to a halt? Would they respect the white hand telling them to stop? Or would they put the pedal to the metal until they'd embedded him like a butterfly on their windshields? He too had been pushing me into this. He was a part of it, together with my brother Miguel, the sergeant with the cat's head spinning through the air, the gears that had been set in motion the night of the storm and that were now pushing my life toward some unknown fate. Clutching the railing I look over at the dull gray apartment blocks where I live. On the fourth floor, the weak glow coming from the nightlamp Miriam uses for reading lights up the window.

Minutes later I open the door, turning the key slowly in the lock, trying to make as little noise as possible. I'm a thief raiding my own house. But the hinges squeak and I'm sure that Miriam has heard me and is waiting. I'm not ready to go in and confront her. My breath quickens, I try to think what to tell her, how to explain it all to her. The seconds go by. Miriam doesn't say anything. Finally, I'm the one who makes a move. When I poke my head inside the door to the bedroom I see that she's lying on her side, her back to me. Asleep, luckily. Always sleeping. Here's my chance to steal what I need without having to explain anything at all. I quickly open the dresser drawer where Miriam keeps important documents. I push aside the marriage papers and take out the passports, leaving hers there and then putting mine in my pocket just as I hear her moving around on the mattress, the squeaking of the bedframe.

"Ulysses…"

I turn around. The outline of a pregnant woman clutching a baby is staring at me.

"Miriam?"

"No, it's me. Claudia," comes a voice that I start to recognize.

I turn to one side so the light from the nightlamp doesn't hit me in the face. I recognize María asleep in her arms.

"What are you doing here?" I ask her, puzzled.

"Alejandro is on duty, so I came to keep Miriam company." Claudia gets out of bed and comes over to me. It's astonishing how much she looks like Miriam.

"Miriam's been looking for you all day."

I step back. I can't bear dealing with anyone I know. For a few seconds I think I've fallen into some kind of trap. That Claudia is really Miriam, and that the baby she has in her arms is our daughter.

"It's not right for Miriam to spend all night at the hospital, as far along as she is…"

"Hospital? What hospital?"

"Heavens!" her hand goes up to her mouth. "Don't you know what's happened?"

"No."

"You don't know about your father?"

34

· · · · · · · · · ·

I enter the hospital by a side door. It's seven forty. Without knowing where I'm going, I walk through the halls. Ever since this craziness started, ever since I decided to leave everything behind, I can't stop noticing clocks. As if time, with its relentless passing, were the only thing that ties me to reality, the only thing that I still have in common with the human beings around me. I don't know how I get to the cafeteria but there they are, I see them behind the glass, gathered around the same table: Miriam, her father Armando, Jorgelina—my enemies. My mother seems to have the same obsession that I do: with her eyes locked onto in the clock hung on one of the walls, she watches the slow movement of its little hands without saying a word. I decide to leave this aquarium-like vision of my family before anyone turns around and surprises me, and I depart.

On the second floor I go into the ward the nurse directs me to. The first thing I notice is the strong disinfectant smell. Standing still, waiting for my eyes to adjust to the weak light, gradually I start to distinguish the rows of beds.

I find my father in the last one. Doubled up in a fetal position, he's hardly a lump underneath the sheets. I kneel down on the cold tiles. His eyes are shut and he's got deep rings of a sickly bluish color under them. It almost makes me take him by the hand instinctively.

"*Patera*," I say, "*Patera.*"

The IV connected to his arm is dripping, drop by drop.

"Pa, I'm leaving now…I'm going to do what you always wanted…I'm going to the United States. Do you hear me? To the U.S.!"

I know it's impossible, my father is only flesh and bones, there's hardly any soul left in that body, but for some unexplainable reason I feel my words are transcending the physical limits separating us and that my father hears me.

The door to the ward opens and Miriam enters.

"I'm leaving now, Pa," I manage to say to him. Behind her, right on the doctor's heels, my mother and Armando come in, too.

There's no time left. I bend down over the old man and kiss him on the forehead. Before they manage to see me—I can't help but feel some shame—I slide underneath the bed like a fugitive. The only things I see now are pantlegs, calves, knees. There are my mother's shoes, actually her old worn slippers, frayed on the sides because of the way she has always dragged her feet, and for a second I lose it. I'm crying, and it takes a huge effort to keep them from hearing my sobs.

Miriam and her father sit down on a small couch, and my mother's slippers draw closer to the bed. She whispers something in Greek that I don't understand until I pay more attention: she is praying. I can't bear the presence of those neglected, twisted fingers any longer; they seem to be telling me to go, telling me not to lose any more time, that we only have one life and there's nothing that justifies wasting it. I slide away, dragging myself along beneath the beds. I dodge around bathrobes hanging down, overturn a bedpan and get splashed by urine, but finally I reach the door. And go out. I turn down a corridor, dodge a nurse pushing an invalid in a wheelchair, and reach the elevators. When the door opens, the first one to step out is my sister Jorgelina. She opens her eyes wide, her lips start trembling, and she holds out her arms as if to put them around me, but I turn around.

"Ulysses!" she screams. "Ulysses!"

Her voice, a whip lashing again and again at my back, pursues me unforgiving as I walk away.

35

. . . .

In only four hours I've succeeded in completely getting rid of my past. I go into Chris's cabin. The sunlight pierces through the porthole with its glorious rays—it's almost a painting by Michelangelo—and the only thing missing to make my triumphal welcome complete are the trumpets of victory. I undress silently, taking off all my clothes, and in a purely instinctive move, open the porthole and throw my things into the water. I look for the alarm clock, for Chris's watch, and take off my own, and let them all fall into the river too. Then, my eye clouded over with fatigue and my ear still throbbing, I lie down next to the fat girl, and for the first time in days I feel I am finally going to be able to go to sleep. Like a survivor who discovers a piece of wood miraculously saved from the shipwreck, I put my arms around her, ready never to let her go, and shut my eyes.

36

· · · · · · · · · ·

The crew of a boat loaded with sand from the industrial port is watching us in envy, with the same resentment that anyone would have, including myself just a few weeks back, at the sight of a bunch of people water-skiing on a weekday in such a carefree way.

To go full speed over the water, feeling the river breeze moving over my whole body while the sun, one of those strong March suns, warms my muscles—it's a more than pleasant sensation. And I'm doing pretty well at it for being my first time.

Doug slows down. I drop gently into the water until I'm just floating there. The boat turns around while I finish getting out of my skis.

"You were perfect!" Chris is bubbling over.

Fred holds out a hand to help me climb up.

"That was really your first time?" Sarah asks suspiciously.

I nod quietly, just as surprised as she is that it seems so easy to me.

"I don't believe it," she insists skeptically. "My father's been trying to teach me to water-ski every since I was two years old, and I still fall."

"Your problem is counterweight," Doug explains, grabbing her breasts like someone tooting a horn. "You're top-heavy!"

Sarah strikes out at him, but Doug dives head first into the water and swims toward the tow-rope handle. The driver's seat is empty. I can't resist the temptation to get in it.

"Can I drive the boat?"

"Of course," Chris says.

"It's not your first time, is it?" Sarah emphasizes with a mocking tone.

"Even if it is," Chris interrupts, "I'm sure he'll do it just fine."

Doug shouts the last instructions while putting on the skis.

"Go slow until the cord is taut, then you can gradually accelerate."

When I see that he's done buckling on the life vest and takes hold of the handle at the end of the rope, ready to go, I put the motor in gear. I accelerate slowly at first until Doug comes up completely out of the water and starts to slide bouncing and see-sawing over the surface. I keep on accelerating, with an eye on Doug until the wind is blowing my hair wildly down over my forehead.

A sailboat comes along next to us. Swaying, with its sails taut from the wind pushing it along, it seems to be urging Doug to show what he can do. Leaning his body to this side and that, concentrating, Doug traces out large *S*'s that remain outlined on the water's surface.

After a breakfast on deck, with a lot of beer, I doze off on one of the deck chairs, lying on my back. Chris spreads suntan lotion on my shoulders. Fred and Sally are sleeping next to each other, and Doug, under a sunshade, is resting with his head on Sarah's stomach. Isabel arrives carrying my orange juice on a tray. Nothing is out of place; this is the way life should be. I rest the frosty glass on my chest and, drowzy from the siesta and the warmth, bring the straw up to my lips. The taste of the freshly squeezed orange is cooling. Chris is caressing my neck. Playfully, negligently, I caress her arm. For a second everything is so calm and peaceful that even the fat girl seems attractive to me. As I fumble for my straw, a strange object looms up in my field of vision, and though I'm still a bit sleepy I know that what I'm seeing ought not to be there. I sit up, alarmed. It's a head, an unexpectedly well known one, dangerously familiar, that is mounting the starboard stairway, dragging after it a body that gets wider and wider.

"Miriam!" I hear myself say the name in my head and then repeat it immediately while coughing through the juice that's choking me. "Miriam!"

It really is my wife, holding up her belly, panting from the climb, standing now next to the railing.

"Uli, is that you?" she asks timidly when she recognizes me shading myself from the sun with my hand. "Is that you?"

Sarah, then Fred, then Susan, then Doug raise their heads, one after the other, like something the reverse of a castle of cards collapsing. Chris is the last to realize the new presence.

"What are you doing here?" my jaw drops.

Before she can answer me, the fat girl sits up belligerently like a buffalo.

"Who IS she?"

Miriam is so surprised that I'm on board the boat, so shocked to see me on that deck covered with lounge chairs, that she doesn't even notice the fat girl's alarm and forges on ahead as if she wanted to make certain of what I cannot explain to her in any way.

"A friend of yours brought me," she gestures confusedly toward the deck below where I think I see Vincent. "He told me you were cheating on me with some other girl, that you were thinking of going away without telling me anything." Inhibited because the others are there, she starts talking like a little kid. "I didn't believe him, I thought it was a joke." But her voice gets more and more precise. "Now that I see you here on this boat, in a bathing suit, touching that girl and..."

Poor Miriam can't take it anymore and her hands come up to her face to hide her tears.

"Who is she?" Chris asks me wildly, and since I don't answer she turns to her friends. "Who is she?"

"Stop, dear," I say, trying to calm her down. "Don't cry anymore..."

But I can't keep treating Miriam like dirt. If we'd been alone, the two of us in the apartment, I would have walked out, slamming the door. But on the deck here I can't leave her by herself, not with so many strangers around that don't even speak the same language. Miriam holds out her hand trying to find something to support herself with, and I grab a deck chair and help her sit down.

"Who is this pregnant woman?" Chris grabs me by the arm and spins me around like a top.

"It's my wife, Chris. My wife!" I realize that I'm destroying everything I've built up, that my image in the fat girl's eyes is melting away like ice cream in the sun, but I can't do anything to stop myself. "Can't you wait a second? Can't you see how she is?"

A violent slap spins my face around. Chris runs down the stairs and I touch my cheek with my hand.

"Chris!" I shout. "Chris! Come back! It's not what you think!"

Down the stairs I run, though with regrets. The fat girl skitters like a rat through the door leading to the staterooms. I follow her. But when I try to go further along the passage, Etta stops me cold, blocking the way by holding her arms out.

"I have orders not to let you through."

"Me?"

Etta nods without saying a word. I can't believe what is happening and so I shout at Chris over her shoulders.

"Chris, please!"

My voice echoes in the corridor, but the fat girl doesn't come out.

"Chris, I can explain everything!"

Etta, disregarding all my yelling, looking down at the floor, stays there with her arms outstretched, blocking the way.

"Chris?!"

Ben bursts out of one of the staterooms, evidently bothered.

"What's all this noise about?" he asks her as if I don't even exist. "I don't want to hear it any more of it, Etta."

I leave the passageway to go up on deck. Down below on the pier Vincent is helping Miriam get into a car. Standing on the stairway leading to the upper deck, Doug, Fred, Susan, and Sarah are staring at me with the same looks they had on their faces when they saw me for the first time, as what I really am: an exotic butterfly they can put back under the glass so it won't bother them, an eccentric person who has passed through their lives to amuse them but who is no longer needed.

37

· · · · · · · · · ·

Back in the apartment everything is turned upside down, broken, lying on the floor, as if a tornado had roared through the narrow space of the two rooms but for some strange reason had left the rest of the building untouched. In the middle of the devastation, seated on the only chair that miraculously has survived the disaster, my mother is breathing, but very still, dejected. The weak light coming in through the window is the last light of afternoon; the room is turning sepulchral. The broken forms look like tombstones, and the pasty air caused by the lack of light makes it seem like being stuck in a cemetery. I stare at everything all spread around, the destruction that Miriam caused, and I stop to look at the self-portrait thrown to the floor along with a photograph of our civil wedding ceremony. The shattered glass prevents the faces from being seen clearly, but you can guess at the features, the glasses raised high for a toast, the shouts of joy. For a few seconds I can almost feel the grains of rice falling down my neck.

"Vincent came to the hospital this morning," my mother's voice interrupts me as I am trying to remove the splintered bits of glass from the frame. "He talked to Miriam."

I succeed in pulling the photograph free. Now that I'm determined to leave, this picture may be the only memento of my children, the twins, that I will have in the future. There's only a slight broadening around Miriam's belly and hips.

"How he's grown, hasn't he?" my mother goes on. "It must be because of the vitamins. He told me that in the United States they take lots of vitamins…And milk, lots of milk…"

She remains silent.

"Miguel, was he bigger or smaller than Vincent?" she looks at me as if we were sitting in the plaza, like retired people.

"Bigger, Mama."

"Really?"

"Much bigger."

I put the photograph in one of my pockets.

"He's a handsome boy, Vincent is. Tall, strong. He told me to let you know that the boat leaves tomorrow. But he's not going to be on it because he's going back with his girlfriend on a plane, he told me. But he left everything ready…"

I go into the bedroom. In the clutter of our closet, I find a small bag.

"You're going away?"

I don't respond. But as I pack a few clothes, the severed head of the cat spinning through the air at the construction sight appears among the coathangers before my eyes, the cat's head flying over me, my brother, and Vincent like an ominous prediction, and I can't help remembering, can't help seeing myself there on the breakwater, shouting foolishly through the wind at Miguel not to go away.

When I go back to the living room my mother is crying silently. With my bag over my shoulder I walk past her toward the door, and when I open it to go out I hear her slippers sliding along, the old slippers so worn along the sides, coming closer to me. I turn. I see her for the last time, silhouetted against a sky heavy with storm warnings, ghostly against the last dim glow coming in through the windows.

"He's dead, Ulysses," she tells me. Her outline blurs, my mother disappears, and the last thing I see is her handbag at her elbow, swinging. "Your father died."

Then I see the cat's head floating there, smiling at me forever, as if it knew that after that night the place my destiny was bringing me to was this one.

38

· · · · · · · · · ·

When I make the last turn of the companionway and enter the galley, leaving behind me the night that is growing over the city, Marco raises the bottle of wine and lets out a huge belch.

"Welcome! Welcome to Disney World, kid!" he shouts at me, trying to get to his feet. "You got your ticket! But it's only one way. Don't think you'll get the round trip, too!"

I step into the water—I'm wondering who the asshole was that took up the planks—and, feet submerged, plow toward the swinging door leading to the little cabins where the bunks are.

"You'll love Mickey Mouse! And you'll have a washing machine." Marco comes over toward me. He splashes everything as he whirls around me laughing with huge guffaws as if he were telling me a funny joke. "And when you go clean the toilets for the guy at the corner and rummage through his shit and he gives you a few bucks you'll go out on the street and holler, 'What a country, macho. I love it!'"

I push him away. "That's enough, Marco."

He staggers as he falls back, arching his back trying to recover his balance like he was on the verge of collapsing completely, but finally he reaches for the swinging door and goes on.

"At night you'll be wiped out and fall into your bed in a cheap hotel with cardboard walls, you'll put earplugs in your ears so the Colombian woman screaming next door because her husband is beating her won't wake you up, and then you'll dream. Oh, will you ever dream, my friend! Even when you don't want to!"

I shove him again, letting all my anger out on him, the hatred I feel toward life because of the shitty destiny it's pushing me toward, and Marco goes through the door and falls down in the water.

"You'll see your country," he keeps talking from the floor, "your friends, some chick that kissed you once…But you'll only see them in your dreams! Because in reality, you'll never ever have enough courage to come back to actually see them!"

When I realize it's my tears that are getting my cheeks wet, I can't stand it anymore and walk out of the galley. I climb up to the bridge and rat on Willy. I know this will make me a traitor, that for the first time in my life I'm doing something that will change me essentially, that I'm crossing a boundary with no chance of return. But it's my only way out, my only possibility of beginning something new, of finally and forever getting rid of the resentment this country fosters in its children. I show the Captain the spot where Willy is hiding the money—I pull at the Playmate of the Month poster on the headboard over his bunk and they just fall out—and then I show them the knife Willy plans to murder José the Panamanian with.

That night neither José nor I sleep. In a filthy engine room, the floor covered with oil, the rumbling muffled by the thickness of the hull, beneath the pitiless light of a bare lightbulb, José beats Willy until he's tired of it. Again and again he brings a leather strap down on the black man's lacerated back. The Captain, seated a few yards away, watches in silence and drains beer cans.

Even though it's raining the next morning, we get under way early. Myself dressed as a sailor next to the Captain, the officer in charge of the wheel, and José the Panamanian smoking a cigarette with a bandaged hand.

"Ulysses," I hear. "At your command, sir." I step up before the Captain.

"Please," his tone is amiable, "you'll have to empty the bilge and throw away those cans."

I fling the empty beer cans into the wake behind the boat. Buenos Aires is dwindling in the distance as we get into the open river. I'm leaving my country the way I set out to do, although several things that belong to me remain buried in this country that is squeezing me out: a brother in the Malvinas Islands, a father who is even at this moment being buried—a man who dreamed his whole life long of living somewhere else—and two children that I never wanted, growing in their mother's belly.

I go back to the bridge and from the window watch the cans scattering in the distance. The Captain finishes the last beer and throws it hard enough so it reaches the water.

"What was it like having a Vietnamese impaled on the end of your knife?" I wonder as I watch the Captain's hands. Even though I don't know the answer, in a flash of absolute revelation—as the city disappears forever behind the horizon—I understand that no one is really pushing me out. That in reality, I, Ulysses, am the last survivor.